PUFFIN

THE WRONG PONG

/ABCL

Steven Butler is an actor, dancer and trained circus performer as well as a keen observer of trolls and their disgusting habits. He has starred in *Peter Pan*, *Joseph and the Amazing Technicolor Dreamcoat*, and as Henry in *Horrid Henry Live* and *Horrid!* His primary school headmaster was the fantastically funny author Jeremy Strong.

Books by Steven Butler

THE WRONG PONG

THE WRONG PONG

STEVEN BUTLER

Illustrated by Chris Fisher

PUFFIN

For Francesca Simon, Rosemary Sandberg
and Elv Moody. Three very squibbly overlings.

PUFFIN BOOKS

Published by the Penguin Group
Penguin Books Ltd, 80 Strand, London WC2R 0RL, England
Penguin Group (USA) Inc., 375 Hudson Street, New York, New York 10014, USA
Penguin Group (Canada), 90 Eglinton Avenue East, Suite 700, Toronto, Ontario, Canada M4P 2Y3
(a division of Pearson Penguin Canada Inc.)
Penguin Ireland, 25 St Stephen's Green, Dublin 2, Ireland (a division of Penguin Books Ltd)
Penguin Group (Australia), 250 Camberwell Road, Camberwell, Victoria 3124, Australia
(a division of Pearson Australia Group Pty Ltd)
Penguin Books India Pvt Ltd, 11 Community Centre, Panchsheel Park, New Delhi – 110 017, India
Penguin Group (NZ), 67 Apollo Drive, Rosedale, Auckland 0632, New Zealand
(a division of Pearson New Zealand Ltd)
Penguin Books (South Africa) (Pty) Ltd, 24 Sturdee Avenue, Rosebank, Johannesburg 2196, South Africa

Penguin Books Ltd, Registered Offices: 80 Strand, London WC2R 0RL, England

puffinbooks.com

First published 2011
006

Text copyright © Steven Butler, 2011
Illustrations copyright © Chris Fisher, 2011
All rights reserved

The moral right of the author and illustrator has been asserted

Set in 13/20pt Baskerville MT Std
Printed in Great Britain by Clays Ltd, St Ives plc

British Library Cataloguing in Publication Data
A CIP catalogue record for this book is available from the British Library

ISBN: 978–0–141–33390–8

www.greenpenguin.co.uk

MIX
Paper from
responsible sources
FSC™ C018179
www.fsc.org

Penguin Books is committed to a sustainable
future for our business, our readers and our planet.
This book is made from Forest Stewardship
Council™ certified paper.

Contents

A Spot of Bother

Every house has problems . . . Some have leaky taps or creaky floorboards, while others have mice in the basement and bats in the attic. Some are just cold or drafty or cramped.

The Brisket family's house was different. Their house had a troll problem.

A big troll problem.

A Thing

In the darkness of a Tuesday night, something wet slopped on to the tiles of the Brisket family's bathroom. It lay there for a minute or two, panting in a puddle of toilet water, before wriggling to its feet and skittering to the door.

Out in the hallway, it skulked across the floor, walking as much on its hands as its feet, and sniffed the air. Ahead were three doors. The stumpy thing pushed the first door and peeked inside.

'BLLLLLEEEEEUUUUURRRRGGGHHH!!'

It was a cupboard filled with clean-smelling sheets and towels. The creature gagged at the stink.

The second door smelled better. Reaching up, the creature turned the handle and pushed.

'Oooooooooooohhhh.'

In the inky darkness its sharp eyes could clearly

see a flowery bedroom where two people were fast asleep in bed.

Snore . . . Grunt . . . Wheeze . . . Snore . . .

The stumpy thing climbed up on to the end of the bed and stalked silently towards the sleeping faces of Marjorie and Herbert Brisket.

Herbert Brisket was snoring the loudest. The creature pushed its nose against him and sniffed. He smelled of aftershave and toothpaste.

'BLEEECCCHHH!!' it grimaced.

Next was Marjorie. The creature stuck its tongue out and licked the end of her nose. She fidgeted in her sleep but didn't wake up. 'Mmmmmmmmmm.' The ladything tasted interesting, like fat and salt and old teabags rolled into one.

The taste was good but not good enough. With one last lick of her cheek, it snorted and jumped on to the dressing table where it tasted all of Marjorie's lotion jars and perfume bottles. It didn't like any of them.

There was a wardrobe against the far wall, and the creature leapt inside to rummage through all sorts of exciting human things. It emerged in a

shower of shoes and jumpers, wearing sunglasses and a pair of Herbert's trousers on its head.

'Oorrrrrrrrrrrrrrrrrrrhhh,' it said, admiring its reflection in the mirror. This was fun.

The creature crept back into the hallway and was just about to open the third door when the Brisket family's dog, a Chihuahua called Napoleon, scampered up the stairs and barked. The creature stalked slowly towards the dog and sniffed, while Napoleon yip-yapped wildly. The creature liked Napoleon's smell of grass and fur and milk, but the third door smelled better still and was a lot less barky, so it picked the dog up, dropped him into the laundry basket and swung the lid shut.

'*Yip, yip, yip,*' the creature imitated, picking up a pair of stray pants from the floor and chewing on them hungrily. '*Yip.*'

The last room was filled from top to bottom with toys and books and all sorts of fantastic new things to taste and play with. It sniffed the air and smelled plastic and paper and chalk and chocolate.

'MMMmmmmmmmmm.'

It ate a pack of wax crayons, tore the pages out of the books and stacked them into a tower.

It unravelled a woollen sweater and threw building blocks at the ceiling.

In a bed in the corner slept Neville Brisket. The creature, still wearing sunglasses and its trouser hat, climbed on to the bed, sniffed Neville and then drew dots on his face with a blue pen from the bedside table. 'Kooooooooooooooooo!' Neville rolled over and snorted.

The creature smacked its hands over its mouth, to keep from squealing. It loved the sound of human snores, they were so funny. Neville snored again. The creature blurted out a big, fat laugh and shoved a stumpy finger up Neville's right nostril.

Yip ... Yip ... Yip ...

Neville woke with a start, flailing his arms and legs. He couldn't see anything without his glasses. If he had been wearing them, he would have noticed a shadowy shape waddle across the room and clamber into the wardrobe. But he wasn't, so he didn't.

Neville reached out and fumbled for his glasses, found them and perched them on his nose. He had a grumbling in the bottom of his belly, telling him that something wasn't quite right. He had been dreaming a finger was up his nose ...

A sour-smelling finger ...

Someone else's sour-smelling finger.

'Yuck!'

Neville was a 'fraidy-cat. He was such a big 'fraidy-cat he was 'fraidier than ten cats all rolled into one big 'fraidy-lion. He was afraid of the dark and of clowns and his grandma Joan and the neighbour's guinea pig, Jeffrey. He jumped every time the microwave went *ding* and when the central heating clicked. He hid when the milkman came to the front door and got upset if different types of food touched each other on his plate. All in all, Neville was scared of everything. He was especially scared of strangers.

What if a stranger was in the house? What should he do? He threw back the blankets and hopped out of bed. *I should wake Mum and Dad and make them search for burglars or bogeymen*, he thought.

At his bedroom door, Neville paused for a moment. *They'll be angry if I wake them up again.* He could hear his mum complaining about having her beauty sleep disturbed and his dad telling him to be a man.

Neville rummaged in the toy-chest at the end of the bed and pulled out his 'handyman torch'. He flicked it on and gasped. His room looked like a herd of elephants had stampeded through it. There was mess everywhere. Mum would be so angry. She hated mess. Something very strange was going on.

'Help,' whimpered Neville. 'Mummy.'

He wanted to run back to bed and hide under the covers but, if he did that, the stranger might go through the house and steal all his toys or, worse, the TV. Walking slowly round the bed, he looked with wide eyes at the tower of ripped books and the torn-off head of his teddy bear.

Who did this? he thought. Neville shone his torch into every nook and cranny but spotted nothing. He was just about to relax when the wardrobe burped. Neville froze. He was pretty sure wardrobes weren't supposed to do that.

'Hello?' he said. 'Is anyone there?' Neville slowly approached the wardrobe door. 'I am brave,' he told himself. 'I am big and brave and there's nothing scary in . . .'

'Yip, yip, yip!'

The noise came from outside in the hallway. Neville spun round with a yelp and headed towards the bedroom door.

Inside the wardrobe, the creature breathed a sigh of relief, then picked its toes and ate what it found between them. Adventuring was hungry work.

The hall was dark and scary-looking and that strange yelping sound made Neville's heart race even faster.

'Be brave,' Neville said to himself. 'Like Captain Brilliant.'

Captain Brilliant was Neville's favourite superhero. He was strong and wore fancy green pants over his tights. Neville wished he had a pair of fancy green pants. He felt sure they would make him braver.

He crept along nervously, keeping near to the wall. When he passed his parents' room he could hear them snoring. He imagined for a moment how great it would be if a robber stole Dad's computer and Mum's magazines. They were always so busy with grown-up things that they often forgot Neville was even there.

'*Yip, yip-yip, yip-yip-yiiiiip!*' There it was again.

The sound seemed to
be coming from the
laundry basket outside
the bathroom.
It sounded like the dirty
clothes had come alive
and were very angry
about something.

He lifted the lid very
slowly. Inside, something
small was running in circles at the bottom of the
basket.

'Napoleon!' Neville snapped in an angry whisper.
He reached inside and lifted the little dog out.
'What are you doing in there?'

Napoleon wriggled and barked in Neville's
hands. He looked like an insane rat with his twiggy
legs running in mid-air.

'Did you make the mess in my room?' Neville
asked angrily. Napoleon just wriggled. 'You scared
me, you rotten dog.' Neville checked to make sure
he was out of earshot and his mum wouldn't hear
him. 'You little poo on legs.' He dropped Napoleon
back into the laundry basket and closed the lid.

'You can stay in there all night.'

Neville was about to head back to bed when his tummy growled loudly. All the nervousness and his mum's extra-healthy cooking was enough to upset anyone's tummy. She had forced him to eat tofu and bean-sprout salad for dinner that day. The tofu was squishy. Neville hated squishy food, and it had been touching the bean sprouts. He headed into the bathroom.

SPLOSH. There was water from the toilet all over the floor, and Neville was standing right in it. 'Napoleon,' he humphed. He dried his foot on one of his mum's favourite towels, dropped his pyjama trousers and sat on the toilet. Finally he could relax . . .

But not for long.

'Pppsssssssstttt,' came a voice. 'You get back down here this instant.'

Neville's jaw dropped. He looked down. The voice was coming from down the toilet.

'I won't be tellin' you again, young man. Your mooma will be spitting beetles if she finds out you came up here by yourself!' With that, a large grey-

green hand shot up and grabbed Neville's thigh. Neville opened his mouth to scream but nothing came out. He grabbed hold of the toilet seat and held on tightly.

'Come on!' the voice said, as the grey-green hand pulled harder. Neville's hands slipped off the edge of the toilet seat and he grabbed at anything he could to stop himself from being pulled downwards. His hand clutched at something cold and metallic and, before he even realized what he had done, he pulled the flush.

There was a great surge and Neville lost his grip. Just as he found his voice to scream, he was swept below the water and could only gurgle. In an instant, Neville and the grey-green hand were gone. Vanished down the toilet.

WHOOOOOOOOOOOOOOOOOOOSSSSHHHH . . .

The Wrong Pong

With a great big whoosh, Neville found himself
falling at a ferocious speed through a foul-smelling,
rusty pipe. The water around him splooshed and
churned as he was spun down into the darkness.

A hefty arm suddenly wrapped itself round
Neville's waist. He squirmed but the arm held tight.

'Up we go,' came a voice behind Neville. He
heard the sound of a chain being grabbed and
he was swung up out of the disgusting water and
into the air.

Neville landed on his belly with a BUMP.
'Oooooof!'

He clambered to his feet, coughing and
spluttering out the rotten taste of toilet before he
was sick. What was going on? Neville started to cry.
He couldn't see anything in the gloom. Mum was
always telling him there were no such things as
toilet monsters and now one had got him.

Somehow, Neville's glasses had managed to stay wedged on his nose, but they were all dirty and smeared with . . . he didn't want to think about what they were smeared with so he quickly wiped them on his pyjama bottoms.

When he put his glasses back on, Neville could see that he was standing in the open mouth of an enormous pipe, high above churning water below him, coming from lots of other pipes. There were little lanterns made from jam jars and milk bottles hanging from the ceiling. Hundreds of them, with drooping wax candles melting and flickering inside each one.

Neville had never been in the sewers before but he was pretty certain there weren't supposed to be lanterns.

'Right, youngling,' boomed a voice. 'Wait till I get my grabbers on you.

What were you thinking, running off like that? You're in big, big trouble.'

Neville spun round. In front of him loomed something from a nightmare. It looked like a human that had been crossed with a knobbly potato or a big old ginger root and was twice as tall as Neville's dad. It was fussing with a batch of ugly-looking fish hanging from a hook on its belt. Neville noticed an empty hook and wondered if it was for him.

'Your mooma would knock you through next-door's back wall if she knew you . . .' The thing looked up and saw Neville in the lantern light. Confusion spread across its face like a rash. 'Who are you?' it asked. Neville couldn't say anything. 'You ain't my youngling! Where's Pong?'

It stormed towards Neville and picked him up as easily as picking up a rag-doll. 'WHERE'S MY YOUNGLING?'

'I-I-I don't know,' Neville stammered. 'I was just using the toilet and you grabbed me.' He started to cry again.

The big thing suddenly looked very ashamed. It put Neville down on the floor of the pipe and sat down beside him.

'Oh, dungle droppings!' it said. 'You mean my little Pong is still up there?'

'I think so,' said Neville. 'I think he tore the head off my bear and put the dog in the laundry basket.'

'That sounds like Pong.' The great big thing grunted. 'Wait till I get hold of him. This is a right pickle.' It put its bucket-sized head in its hands. 'I'm in trouble.'

'W-w-what are you?' Neville asked. 'Are you a toilet monster?'

The thing glared. 'No! They're disgusting,' it said. 'I'm a troll.'

'A troll?' said Neville. 'I thought trolls only live under bridges.'

The troll scoffed. 'Rubbish,' it said. 'Far too much daylight. We like it all dark and dooky.'

'Well, Mister Troll,' said Neville. 'I have an idea. Why don't you just take me back and collect your Pong all in one go? My parents will still be asleep. No one will know.'

The troll shook his head. 'That's just it,' it said. 'I can't. It's the law.'

'What law?' Neville didn't like the sound of that.

'Troll law. We can only go up the toilet on special grab nights. With the help of a wee smidge of troll magic the pipes go all stretchy and we can climb up to the overlings' world. We can't go up now, it's too late.'

'Please take me home. PLEASE!' Neville wailed. This was terrible. He was stuck in a sewer that smelled a million times worse than the school toilets with a giant troll.

'Pong is stuck up there now, and you're stuck down here. There's no use gripin' in the pipin'. You'll just have to get used to it.'

Neville looked ready to cry.

'I'm Clod,' said the troll, extending a hand in Neville's direction. 'Clod Bulch.'

It stepped into the light of the candles and smiled. Its skin was the colour of old lettuce, with patches of earthy brown and dirty grey freckles. Its eyes were bright like pennies and its mouth stretched across its face like a crack in a lumpy pavement, and it was surrounded with thick beardy bristles. The top of its head was bald except for a few nasty-looking mushrooms growing there like stowaways. It was a fright to behold.

'I'm Neville,' said Neville. 'Brisket, Neville
Brisket.' Clod pulled a face.

'You overlings call each other strange things.'
He scooped Neville up in his big arms and swung
him round on to his back.
'I'd better take you to
meet the Mooma.'

With that, Clod
galumphed off with
Neville clinging to
his shoulders,
whimpering softly.
Neville closed his
eyes tight and
prayed that this was
all just a dream . . .
A very smelly dream.

Meanwhile

The sun rose as usual in the world above and the thing called Pong was having a brilliant time bending the forks and spoons in the kitchen drawers.

Herbert and Marjorie were up and about, but they were far too busy with their computers and gossiping and magazines to notice that anything was wrong.

'AAAAAAAAAARRRGGGHHHHHHHH!!' yelled Pong, and threw a twisted teaspoon across the room. It bounced off the back of Herbert's head.

'Don't do that, Neville,' Herbert said.

Pong grunted and put the fruit bowl into the microwave.

Underneath

Clod carried Neville deep underground through smelly pipes and passageways, trudging for what seemed like hours, until they passed through a stone arch with the words 'WELCOME UNDER' carved across the top. Suddenly there were lots of trolls, like Clod, hithering and thithering in all directions. One or two caught sight of Neville on Clod's back and gasped as they hurried on their way, holding their noses.

A troll with a face covered in nettles and warts came out of a door in the wall and stopped Clod. He pointed to Neville.

'Wassat you got there?' he asked.

'He's called Neville,' said Clod.

'What's a Neville?' asked Nettle-face. 'Poo, he stinks of clean.' The weeds growing like a beard on his chin twitched angrily.

'He's a rare breed,' said Clod, thinking quickly.

'He got swapped with my Pong so he's mine now till I can put him back or swap him. Them's the rules.'

The troll looked at Neville suspiciously. 'Don't seem natural,' he said. 'I've never heard of a Neville in these parts. Whatever it is, it's weird and don't half smell.'

'You're the one with weeds on his face,' said Neville, before he remembered to remember he was a 'fraidy-lion. 'And I don't smell . . . YOU DO!' Then he instantly ducked back behind Clod's head.

'Steady, Nev,' Clod chuckled. 'We don't want everyone knowing there's an overling about. Next thing you know, everyone'll be wanting one.' He pushed past the nettle-faced troll and plodded into the busy streets beyond.

Neville could hardly believe his eyes and ears. They were in a town. An actual underground town. It was one big, dark, noisy, clangy, rumbly, smoky rubbish dump. Everything was made from old junk. In the light of a thousand flickering lanterns, he saw shops and houses of all shapes and sizes, made from metal railings and twisted car parts, crumbly bricks and cardboard, tin cans and rope, sticks, string, boxes and mud.

'Lovely, isn't it?' said Clod proudly. He couldn't see Neville trembling behind him.

They passed under a colossal junk contraption with a face like a clock. Strangely, the numbers went all the way up to seventy-three and there were hundreds of hands ticking in both directions all over it. There were pendulums swinging this way and that and Clod had to duck as one hurtled past.

TICK . . . DING . . . TICK . . . DING . . . TICK . . . DING . . . It was so noisy it hurt Neville's ears.

'What's that?' asked Neville, gripping tightly.

'That,' said Clod, 'is the ticker-dinger-thinger. It's very important.'

'Ooooh,' said Neville. He tried to read it but, with so many hands and numbers, it was impossible. 'What does it do?'

'It tells the time, of course,' said Clod. 'It was built long ago by trolls that ain't around these parts no more. All we know is that it goes "BANG" when it's get-up time, "BONG" when it's sleep time and every now and again it goes "BOOM". That means it's grab time.'

'Grab time?' said Neville. 'When will the next grab time be?'

'Who knows,' Clod said. 'It makes its own mind up. Once, it took so long the nettles grew all the

24

way up to my noggin. We were all starvatious.'

'That sounds like a long time,' Neville whimpered.

'Oh, it was,' said Clod. 'Awful long wait.'

Neville's heart sank as Clod galumphed further into town.

'Almost there,' Clod said.

'Where are we going?' Neville whispered in Clod's ear.

'Washing Machine Hill,' said Clod. 'It's not far.' And it wasn't. They turned around the corner by a shop displaying a big sign that said 'LEFT SOCK SALE' in red letters, and headed up a steep hill made from broken washing machines.

Halfway up the path the pair came across a
haggard troll lady heading towards them. She
looked older than anything Neville had seen before.

'That's Gristle Pilchard. Don't move
a minch,' Clod whispered to Neville as they got
closer. 'Evenin', Mrs Pilchard,' he said.

'Evenin'. What's that dangling about your neck,
Clod Bulch?' she said, squinting through a pair of
glass-plate spectacles. 'Scarf, is it?' She poked at
Neville's arm with the end of her walking stick.

'Errrrm . . . S'right . . . It's a new kind of scarf. Extra thick to keep the chills out,' Clod lied. Mrs Pilchard poked Neville again.

'Don't sound very comfy if you ask me. Sounds nasty and knotted and it stinks,' she said. 'Let me have a feel.' She reached out her gnarled hand but Clod stepped aside before she could grab Neville.

'Sorry, Mrs Pilch, I'm rushin' and runnin' like a late lump.' Clod hurried past and continued up the path. 'Phew . . . We'll never get rid of her if she finds out about you.'

Neville looked back at Mrs Pilchard, leaning on her stick and watching them hurry up the hill.

'Nosier than an armful of bogeys,' said Clod.

The Jam-Jar House

At the top of the hill, Neville saw a house made entirely from row after row of stacked-up jam jars.

'Here we are.' Clod put Neville down among the piles of washing-machine parts. 'This way, boy,' he said, leading the way.

Neville stepped carefully among the rubbish, trying his hardest to put his feet in the same places that Clod had stepped but his legs weren't long enough.

Just as he was catching up to Clod, something fat and black and furry launched itself at Neville.

'GGGGGRRRRROOOOOAAAARRR!'

It landed against Neville's belly and he toppled to the floor, waving his legs around like an upturned tortoise.

'Good boy, Rabies,' said Clod. 'Play nicely.'

Neville looked up at a giant mole thing scowling down at him with crazed eyes that darted about in all directions.

28

'Get it off me!' yelled Neville. Rabies growled even louder.

'Oh, he don't mean no nevermind,' said Clod, picking the mole off Neville's belly. 'He just wants to play, don't you, Rabies?'

Clod fished inside a pocket and pulled out a plump earthworm. Rabies instantly stopped growling and started licking Clod's face. 'There's a good moley.'

Neville clambered back to his feet and brushed himself off. He watched as Clod put Rabies down and the mole scampered inside the house. Through the jam-jar walls, Neville could see a huge shape clattering around inside. It looked like a hippopotamus in a dress with too much hair. *That must be the Mooma*, he thought, crossing all his fingers and toes and hoping she wasn't hungry.

There was no door in the doorframe at the front of the house. Instead, there hung a dirty green curtain. Clod pushed through it and went inside to plant a sloppy kiss on the Mooma's cheek.

'Hello, my brandyburp,' Clod said. 'I've got a surprise for you.' Then he turned and clomped back towards the curtain. 'Look what I snaffled!'

Neville gave a little whimper as the massive woman turned and stared at him with a look that resembled his own mother's face when she'd discovered that Napoleon had pooed in her slippers again.

'Neville,' said Clod. 'Meet the Mooma.'

Neville held his breath and tried his best not to wet his pants. The Mooma was even bigger than her husband and twice as scary. She was puffing on a long, clay pipe and smoke wisped from her nostrils like a dragon.

'Eeuurrrrgh, what's this?' she said, marching towards Neville and poking a sausage-sized finger into his chest. 'You said you were bringing sewer fish home for dinner, Clod. I'm not eating that.'

The Mooma

'He ain't dinner,' Clod laughed, to Neville's relief. 'He's Neville.'

'Who? Where's the other one? What was his name?'

'Pong,' said Clod.

'Pong, that's it. Where's Pong?'

Neville watched her pick at a toadstool growing on her elbow. She broke off a piece, popped it in her mouth and squelched it slowly between her yellow teeth.

'He got swapped,' said Clod. 'We have a Neville now.'

'You're tellin' me you've brought the wrong Pong?' she hissed. 'Swapped? What rot.'

'It was dark,' said Clod sheepishly.

'You're a troll,' she said. 'You can see in the dark. You could have got a bigger one, Clod. He's scrawnier than a hinkapoot.'

'That's the only size he came in,' said Clod.

She sighed. 'Well, you'll just have to do then, won't you?' She bent down until her potato-sized nose was almost touching Neville. He closed his eyes and prayed to Captain Brilliant.

Clod nudged Neville from behind, sending him sprawling. 'Go on,' Clod said. 'This is Malaria. Ain't she grumptious?'

Neville couldn't speak. He had been afraid before but this was the most scared he'd ever been. Instead, he started opening and closing his mouth like a fish. The Mooma was just so scary, like a boulder in a wig . . . a boulder that ate bits of toadstool growing on its elbows. Yuck!

'I think you've got me a broken one, Clod,' she said. 'There's nothing worse than a broken Neville . . . I've heard.'

'It ain't broken, you dungle!' said Clod.

'Well, it looks broken to me,' she said. 'It's quieter than Pong though. That might be nice.'

'I . . . I . . . I . . .' said Neville, doing his best to gather up all of his courage. If the Mooma thought he was broken she might throw him out, and that could be even worse. Inside there was only Clod and Malaria, but out there were hundreds of huge, scary, child-eating trolls.

'Ssshhhh!' said Clod. 'It's doing something.'

'I-it . . . it's . . . nice to meet you,' said Neville. 'I-I'm Neville. I-I-I WANT TO GO HOME!' Neville burst into tears.

The Mooma smiled, showing her wonky teeth. For a horrible second Neville thought she was going to hug him. Instead she just stretched and belched loudly. Neville almost fainted from the smell.

'Oh, you poor pluglet,' she said. 'I know exactly what will make you happy as a hump-honker.'

Happy? thought Neville. *I've been yanked down the toilet in the middle of the night by a troll. I couldn't possibly be happy . . . unless . . . unless . . .*

He looked up into her orange eyes. Was this it? Was this the moment she would say he could leave the stinky world of underneath and go back to his home and his bedroom and all his toys and books?

'You want a lovely big sister troll to make you feel all safe and squelchy.'

Neville's blood ran cold. There was another troll in the house? After the shock of Clod and Malaria, he wasn't sure he could cope with a third. He curled his toes under, clenched his bottom and braced himself for another scare.

Meanwhile

Pong sat in a chair wearing Neville's school uniform and rocking backwards and forwards. Herbert sipped a glass of wine and Marjorie picked greedily at her dinner while talking to her best friend on the phone.

Pong picked up the roast chicken from the centre of the table and threw it at the ceiling.

'Neville,' snapped Marjorie, without looking up from her plate. 'Behave.'

Pong belched loudly and cooed to himself.

Rubella

Malaria picked up a dusty old broom from the corner and banged on the ceiling with the end of it. 'Belly!' she bellowed.

Neville listened to a heavy pair of feet clomp across the floor above, then the sound of a door banging open.

'I'M NOT COMING DOWN!' screamed a girl's voice.

Clod leaned over to Neville. 'That's Rubella,' he said, gesturing at the ceiling. 'She's . . . like her mother.'

Malaria banged on the ceiling again. 'YOU GET YOUR RAMBUNKING LITTLE RUMP DOWN HERE NOW, YOUNG LADY!'

'NO!' came the voice from upstairs.

Malaria took an enormous breath and let out the loudest 'NOOOOOOOOWWWWWWW!!' Neville had ever heard. It was so loud the whole house trembled and cups and plates started dancing about the table.

Neville held his breath and waited to see what would happen next. Surely no one in the universe would be brave enough to disobey Malaria?

CRASH . . . A head burst through the ceiling in a shower of plaster and bits of jam jar. Neville gasped. It was the ugliest troll face he had seen yet. Even Clod and Malaria looked a little shocked.

'WHAT?' screeched the head. Rubella scowled down at her mooma and dooda. 'I SAID I'M NOT COMING . . .'

Her eyes met Neville's. 'What's that? I'm not eating that.' Neville hid behind Clod's leg and prayed she meant what she said.

'Come down, you nogginknocker,' said Clod, pointing a finger up at his hideous daughter. 'Nev's not for dinner.'

'This is,' said Malaria. She reached over to a pot

on the stove and pulled out what looked like a giant chicken nugget and held it up to the grey-green girl in the ceiling. 'If you don't eat it, we will.'

'WAIT!' Rubella barked and vanished back up through the hole. Neville listened as the great, slobbering girl thundered out of her room and down the stairs. A shudder tingled its way down his spine. *This is it*, he thought.

Rubella emerged at the bottom of the stairs and darted towards the dinner table. She was the ugliest thing Neville had ever seen. Her face was like a smacked bottom covered in boils and pimples, while her eyes were too close together and looked like shrivelled rabbit droppings. Her yellow teeth stuck out like gravestones from behind a droopy bottom lip and she was chubbier than both her parents rolled into one. Where Clod and Malaria had toadstools growing across their necks and shoulders, Rubella had great big turnips sprouting. She smelled like rotten vegetables and mouldy meat and wore a stained dress made from an old bed sheet. Neville recognized the blue background and pink fish pattern instantly. It was one of Marjorie's old bed sheets that went missing long ago.

'FOOD!' Rubella shouted, swatting Neville out of the way like a tiny mosquito. Then she plonked herself down and started opening all the different pots and pans that Malaria had set out. It was like she hadn't even noticed Neville. He clambered nervously on to a chair next to Malaria and did his best not to stare as she shovelled fistfuls of food into her drooling mouth.

'Ha ha,' beamed Clod, clapping his hands. 'Now you've met Rubelly . . . sort of . . . let's eat.'

Dinnertime

'Just wait till you try this,' Malaria said. 'Your tastebudlings will jump a jig. Open wide.'

Neville suddenly thought of Hansel and Gretel being fed up until they were juicy and plump enough to be roasted. He clamped his mouth shut.

'Try it, Nev,' Clod said from the other side of the table. 'It's good.'

'I don't eat green things,' Neville groaned.

'It's not green, is it?'

'Nope,' said Malaria.

The food smelled curious and his tummy was grumbling . . . maybe . . . 'Maybe just this once,' Neville said and stuck out his tongue. He watched as Malaria lifted the lid of one of the pots, then fished around inside for something. She placed one hand over Neville's eyes and then a small chunk of food on his tongue. 'What d'ya think of that?' she asked, taking her hand away from his eyes.

Neville chewed the lump of meat. It tasted like a beef burger but juicier and a little salty. 'It's good,' he said, nodding as he chewed.

'Have another piece,' said Malaria. Neville had another bite. The meat was much better than his mum's parsley soufflé.

'What is it?' asked Neville between mouthfuls.

'Rat patty fried in hair grease,' she said, beaming. 'It's a Bulch family speciality.'

Neville froze, then turned white, then green. He spat the rat patty halfway across the room, jumped up from the table, then yelped and scraped at his tongue with the back of his hand.

'RAT!' he shouted. 'I CAN'T EAT RAT!'

Clod and Malaria looked shocked. Even Rubella stopped scoffing and stared at him for a moment.

'What's wrong with rat?' Malaria asked.

'RAT! IT'S RAT! THAT'S WHAT'S WRONG!'

'It's not wrong . . . It's delicious,' said Malaria.

'BUT IT'S RAT! DIRTY SCURRYING NIBBLING RAT! EEEERRRRRRRRRR!!'

Clod and Malaria stared with wide eyes at

Neville as his face got redder and redder. He started looking like a tomato.

'IT'S DISGUSTING!' he screamed.

'But you said it was good,' said Clod, looking hurt.

'YES BUT . . .' Neville stopped. He suddenly felt very rude indeed. Maybe he should give it one more go.

Neville picked up another rat patty and eyed it suspiciously. He was so hungry, so hungry but . . .

'I'm sorry,' he said, sitting back at the table. 'I'm . . . um . . . just not in the mood for rat at the moment.' Neville smiled a nervous smile. Not knowing what to do with the greasy lump, he stuffed it into his pyjama pocket and tried to ignore the oil oozing down his leg. He'd get rid of it when no one was looking.

'Oh,' said Clod. 'Why didn't you say so?'

'Yes,' said Malaria. 'There's lots of other lummy things to sink your chompers into.'

Neville crossed his fingers and toes and hoped there would be no more nasty surprises. He felt sure there would be something he could eat without turning green.

'Great,' he said.

'Right, my little fussing lump.' Malaria started

removing all the lids and tossing them to the floor. 'We have battered badger lightly sprinkled with verruca shavings. Very nice that one.'

Neville's jaw dropped open. Malaria didn't notice and continued removing lids.

'This is left sock stew,' she said.

'Socks?' asked Neville, who was sure he must have heard wrongly.

'Left socks,' corrected Malaria.

'Left socks?' asked Neville. 'Why only left ones?'

'There's no stronger cheese in the world than toe cheese from an overling's left foot,' said Clod. 'It's not always too easy to get near their feet so we take all the left socks instead. It's just as good. Left sock stew is a cheesy tummy-tinkler.' He licked his lips.

Neville's stomach bubbled. He wished he hadn't asked. What could he try without upsetting the Mooma? He pointed to a tray of brown, square things that looked like blocks of fudge. Neville liked fudge. He could easily eat that.

'What's that?' he asked.

'Ear-wax brownies,' said Malaria. 'Dig in, Nev, they're warm.'

From Bad to Worse

Neville almost threw up.

When the Bulches had finished eating, Rubella clomped back upstairs while Clod and Malaria started to lick the plates clean, ready to go back in the cupboard. They looked like they enjoyed washing up just as much as eating.

BOOOOOOONNNNNNNNGGGGGGG! The ticker-dinger-thinger echoed across the town.

'Right,' said Malaria, licking the back of the last spoon with her slobbery tongue. 'Bong means beddie-byes. We've got market in the morrow.'

Clod yawned loudly. 'I'm pooped,' he said. 'Carrying overlings is tricksy work.'

'You must be snoozed down to your toots,' Malaria said to Neville. She picked up the broom handle and banged on the ceiling. An eye appeared at the hole in the ceiling.

'WHAT?' screeched Rubella.

'This,' said Malaria, pushing Neville under the hole, 'is Neville, remember? He's going to be sharing your room with you while he's here.'

Neville's blood turned to ice. He couldn't sleep in the same room as that . . . that . . . monster. She was a child-eater for sure.

'NO IT'S NOT! I WON'T LET IT IN!' screamed Rubella.

'You'll do as you're told, young lady,' said Clod, puffing up his chest.

'Don't you fret, Nev,' said Malaria. 'We'll make you up a warm place to sleep in Rubella's room. She's a good girl really. Very friendly.' Before Neville could even whimper and imagine Rubella splattering him under her big, angry feet, the trolls swept him up the stairs.

Neville knocked softly on Rubella's door. There was no answer.

'She must be asleep,' he said. 'I don't want to wake her.'

Malaria tutted and pushed the door open. 'The little madam never answers,' she said. Then she pushed Neville through the door and closed it behind him. 'Night, Nev.'

Neville stumbled into the room and fell flat on his face. His spectacles spun off his nose and rattled across the floor. He lay silent for a moment, listening to the sound of Clod and Malaria plodding off to bed. Was this it? Was this the moment Rubella, the dragon-monster, would grab him and tear him to bits?

Neville fumbled around and retrieved his glasses, popped them on and opened one eye. He instantly wished he hadn't.

He found himself staring straight at the hairy big toe of Rubella's large grey-green foot.

'You ain't sleepin' in my hammock,' came her voice from somewhere above him. 'You whimpering little snot.'

'O-OK,' Neville said to the foot.

'And don't talk unless I talks first.'

Neville nodded.

'And if I see you touchin' any of my things I'll pull your hands off. Got it?'

'Got it,' Neville whimpered.

'Get up,' said Rubella.

Neville nervously stood up. For a moment he wasn't sure if he was going to be able to, his knees were trembling so ferociously.

'Eeuurrrgh, ain't you funny-lookin',' said Rubella.

Neville almost laughed. *Him*, funny-looking?

'Stay out of my way,' she growled. Rubella shoved Neville aside and climbed into her hammock. 'You overlings think you can wiffle your way down here and steal our bedrooms . . . WELL, YOU CAN'T!' She slumped herself down and started reading her *Troll Teen* magazine.

Neville was so afraid of making Rubella angry he decided the best thing he could do was stand very, very still and say absolutely nothing. He closed his eyes and tried to imagine being exactly like one of the statues in the park near his home. Maybe that could be his super power. Neville the Statue-boy.

Rubella threw her magazine at him. It bounced off the top of his head and hit the wall. THWACK!

'Stop being so still, you whelp.'

Neville retrieved his glasses from the floor for a second time then started to wriggle and jiggle like a worm in a frying pan.

'Is this better?' he asked between bobs and twists. Rubella turned purple.

'STOP SQUIRMING!' she screamed.

Neville stopped.

'Thank you for letting me stay in your room,' he said. 'It's ever so nice.' He thought if he was extra friendly she might warm to him a little.

'Shut your rat hole,' said Rubella and pointed to a pile of revolting, dirty laundry in the corner of the room. 'You sleep there.'

Neville ran at the laundry pile. Dirty or not, at

least he could hide in there and not look at the warty, knobbly rhinoceros who kept shouting at him.

But as he ran, Neville's foot slipped through the hole in the floor that Rubella had punched earlier in the evening. He tumbled down as both legs vanished beneath him. Oh no, he was stuck in the hole! Rubella pointed and burst out laughing.

'Help me,' Neville whimpered. His legs were kicking wildly at the kitchen ceiling but his body would not budge. 'Please, Rubella.'

'Night, Nev,' Rubella said with a wicked leer. 'Sleep tight, won't you?' Then she slumped down into her hammock and fell quickly asleep, leaving Neville stuck as tight as an elephant in a mole hole.

It was going to be a very long night.

Meanwhile

Pong couldn't understand why the sofa wouldn't fit into the fridge. Marjorie's hat fitted into the oven and Herbert's computer easily went up the chimney.

He scratched his head, then smiled and wobbled off to the bathroom. He spent the morning unravelling all the toilet rolls instead . . .

The Next Day

BAAAAAAAAANNNNNNNGGGGGGG! The ticker-dinger-thinger echoed across the underground cavern.

Neville woke to the worst case of pins and needles he'd ever had. For a moment he couldn't quite remember where he was. He felt dizzy and very, very hungry. Then the whole horrible truth rushed back to him. His legs were still stuck in the hole and they tingled all over like hundreds of ants nipping, jabbing and biting.

Neville looked around the room. Rubella was gone. *That's one bit of good news,* he thought. The door was open and the sickly, sticky scent of some vile troll breakfast wafted up from downstairs. Clod and Malaria must have seen his legs coming through the kitchen ceiling – why hadn't they raced up to help him?

'HELP!' Neville screamed, kicking his legs backwards and forwards. 'HELP!'

'Oh, you're up,' Clod said from the kitchen below. Neville listened as Clod's heavy stomps crossed the kitchen and headed up the stairs. A moment later he appeared at Rubella's door. 'You overlings sleep in some oddly places.'

'I didn't choose to sleep here,' Neville snapped, forgetting to be scared for a moment. 'I fell and not one of you . . . you . . . trolls helped me.'

'Steady on there, Nev,' said Clod, plucking Neville from the hole and lifting him on to his shoulders. 'You'll blow a fuse in your noggin if you start yellin' and accusatin'. We thought, what with you overlings being so weird, you might like sleepin' where you were.' He carried Neville down the stairs and put him on one of the upturned barrels. Rubella was sitting opposite him and sneered.

'Morning,' she hissed. 'Sleep well?'

'Busy day for us today,' Clod said with a grin. 'The market's a squibbly, bundling type of place. Lots to see and lots to do.'

Neville sat on the barrel and rubbed his legs, coaxing the blood to start flowing again.

'We're going to market?' he said.

''S'right,' said Clod.

'To buy things?' Neville asked.

'Good gracicles, no,' said Clod. 'Us trolls don't buy, we swap. We'll swap anythin' and everythin' that can be swapped. As long as it's useful, there'll be someone as wants it.'

Malaria came over from the stove and plonked a bowlful of pickled fish eyes in front of Neville. He choked back the sick that glugged in his throat and pushed the bowl away.

'Eat up, chubbling,' she coaxed. 'It's lummy.'

'I don't want to,' said Neville and folded his arms.

'You've got to eat if you want to grow up big and brawny,' she said. Neville ignored her. A terrible thought crept in at the back of his mind.

'What are you going to swap?' he asked.

'Ooooh,' said Clod. 'All the things we got our hands on last night. There's always a market after a good grabbin'.'

'But,' Neville said, turning a little pale, 'I'm what

56

you grabbed last night. Are you going to swap me?'

'We have to,' said Clod. 'It's the grabber's law. Everything we grab has to be taken to market to swap . . . EVERYTHING.'

'Oooooh, Clod,' said Malaria. 'Remember when Dribble Hacklebottom brought back that goat? Oh, the screamin' and snatchin'.'

Neville gripped the edge of the table so tightly his knuckles turned blue. A vision of himself being tugged in all directions by a mob of hysterical trolls flashed before him. *I have to escape*, thought Neville. *I have to . . . I HAVE TO!*

'But we don't want no one swiping our brand-new Neville. If we lose him we can't switch our Pong back. We'd better take a few extra fish to swap and hope no one catches sight of the wee grub,' said Clod.

'We'll think of somethin',' said Malaria.

'If you take that thing to the market,' said Rubella, pointing a stubby finger at Neville, 'I ain't goin'. I'm not being seen with that oversized foozle dropping.' She hooked an apple-sized bogey from her nostril and flicked it at him. 'FOOZLE DROPPING!'

The Market

A pillowcase. A grotty stained pillowcase that
stank of troll hair-grease and mildew was the best
disguise Clod and Malaria could come up with.

Neville stumbled along at Malaria's side,
snivelling to himself as they bundled downhill
into the town. He peered through the eyeholes

Clod had made in the pillowcase and wanted to cry at the sight of so many trolls coming and going.

'Keep up, Nev,' Clod called from up ahead. 'Not far now.'

'Yeah, keep up, Nev,' said Rubella from behind, jabbing him in the shoulder. 'The sooner we're there, the sooner you're swapped.'

'Shut up, chubby,' Neville mumbled to himself.

'What?' Rubella grunted.

'Nothing.'

The busy town square was heaving with market stalls. Trolls rushed in all directions with armfuls of

paper clips, boxes and bottles and called out from their garbage stands about the great quality of their grabbed goods.

Neville caught sight of the ticker-dinger-thinger but still couldn't work out the time. He made sure to remember the route through the town, despite it being so dark and shadowy. He'd need to know where he was going when he escaped.

The Bulches and Neville wandered through the walkways between stalls. They found an empty stall in the far corner of the square as far away from the crowd as possible. It was wobbly and lopsided but Malaria insisted it would look squibbly with a few fish hung here and there.

'S'pect you've never seen anything like this, eh, Nev?' she said, hooking sewer fish and long, grey eels along the top of the stall. Neville shook his head inside the pillowcase. He looked like a little ghost.

Before long, the fish were laid out and a few straggling customers wandered over to barter and trade.

'Get your sewer fish,' Clod yelled. 'Fresh from the waters of the rustiest pipes.'

'Salty eels,' Malaria joined in. 'Guaranteed to wriggle inside your belly.'

Neville cowered at the side of the stall and tried to look as inconspicuous as possible. He quietly watched tall, skinny trolls with sticks and brambles growing out of their shoulders and short, stumpy trolls with mossy faces and skin like rock. One troll woman was even covered from head to toe in spikes like a cactus. She swapped a ball of yarn for an eel.

Clod had put Neville in charge of stacking up the swapped items behind the stall so no one would notice him. It wasn't easy though. Trying to stack things with your hands inside a pillowcase was tricky business.

The pillowcase smelled very bad, but Neville felt safe inside it and no one paid him any real attention. He supposed if someone could walk around with cactus spikes sticking out of their face, the sight of a pillowcase with legs wasn't too shocking after all. Maybe he wouldn't get swapped.

'Belly, get over here and watch the stall. Me and your mooma are going for a quick nettle tea break,' bellowed Clod.

Rubella had been mooching about a short way

away with a gang of equally nasty-looking teen
trolls. They kicked and scuffed at the grubby earth
as they droned to each other about how hard it was
to be them and how their parents didn't
understand.

Rubella glowered at Neville and curled the ends
of her mouth downwards like she had just
swallowed a stink bug. She lumbered to the stall,
her two friends trailing behind her.

'We won't be long, Belly,' said Malaria, walking
away. 'Neville, you stay out of sight.'

'Belly . . . Belly,' teased one of Rubella's friends.
She was shorter and bonier than Rubella with a

head full of bristly, twiggy hair that creaked every time she moved.

'Shut up, Gruntilda,' snapped Rubella. Gruntilda giggled even harder.

Rubella's other friend, Thicket, who had a thorn briar growing out of his back and a bolt through his left nostril, leaned over the stall and looked at Neville. Neville shrank back.

'What's that?' he asked. 'Eeeeeeuurrrgh.'

Rubella gasped. What would Thicket, the grimiest, thorniest boy in town, think if he knew there was an overling living with her?

'Oh nothing, Thicket,' she said, blushing. 'It's just . . . erm . . . our new pet. Mooma and Dooda swapped it for . . . a squished squirrel.'

'Grotsome,' said Thicket. 'Totally grotsome.'

'It looks weird,' said Gruntilda. 'Your family would swap any old rubbish.'

'Shut up, Gruntilda,' snapped Rubella a second time. 'Your family haven't even got a pet.'

'Yeah, well, that's only cos we don't want one. Look at it,' Gruntilda said. 'It looks like a walking pillowcase.'

'It's a . . . sack beast,' said Rubella.

'It's ugly,' said Gruntilda, giggling.

'Fine,' said Rubella. 'We're getting rid of it anyway.'

Neville, who had been humming the Captain Brilliant theme tune and doing his best to ignore them, froze. What was she going to do?

'I'm swapping it for something more . . . grotsome,' said Rubella, batting her crusty eyelids at Thicket.

Rubella grabbed Neville and hauled him, pillowcase and all, on to the market stall. He landed with a bump among the fish guts and stinking eel skins.

'PET FOR SWAP,' bellowed Rubella. 'GET YOUR OBEDIENT PET TODAY. ONLY ONE IN STOCK.'

Neville wriggled inside the pillowcase. What was he going to do now? If Rubella swapped him, he'd be done for. His nerves wouldn't be able to take it.

A weaselly-looking troll sidled up next to the stall.

'Mmmmm,' he said. 'Mmmmm indeed. You seem to have a very interesting item on your stall.'

'It's a sack beast,' said Rubella. 'They're very obedient and loving.'

'Mmmmm,' said the weaselly troll. 'Mmmmm indeed. It looks meaty and I'm awfully hungry.'

'Going very cheap,' Rubella added. The troll twitched his warty fingers and gave Neville a prod.

'Ooooow!' Neville yelped. 'Hands off.' He wanted to scream and run in circles and not stop until he woke from this terrible nightmare. How could Rubella sell him to the weaselly troll knowing that he wanted to eat Neville? Rubella was a monster.

'Mmmmm,' said Weasel-pants. 'I'm awfully tempted. I'm almost drooling.'

'Well, it will cost you . . . two nails and a bucket,' said Rubella.

'*It will cost you what?*' said Clod, arriving back at the stall with a cracked mug filled with nettle tea. He glared at Rubella. 'What are you doing?' he grunted angrily. 'Do you want everyone to know we've got an overling in our house?'

Then Clod turned to the weaselly troll. 'It ain't for swap. Now bug off!'

The weaselly troll stormed off through the market shouting that he'd never seen such time-wasting in his life. Clod turned to Rubella who shrank away from him. Gruntilda and Thicket ran away laughing.

'Don't you ever let me catch you doing something like that again, young lady – we could have been found out,' he said, pulling Neville down from the stall. 'We'd be laughing stocklings. There'll be no fourths at dinner for you tonight.'

Rubella turned purple. 'You're the meanest dooda in the world! I hate you,' she screamed.

When Clod's back was turned, Rubella bent down to Neville's height, picked off a turnip from her shoulder and squished it on Neville's head. In a tiny whisper that her dooda couldn't hear, she said, 'I'll get you.'

Meanwhile

Marjorie turned round from the sink and screamed as Napoleon trotted happily into the kitchen with lipstick drawn all across his face and a glove on his tail.

'NEVILLE!' Marjorie shouted. 'STOP DRAWING ON THE DOG!'

Neville didn't answer. But a toilet roll sailed through the kitchen door and landed in the sink with a *sploosh*.

'NEVILLE!'

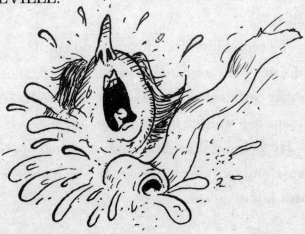

Think of Captain Brilliant

That night in Rubella's room, Neville woke up
curled underneath a pair of very large and very
smelly knickers. He'd been running from trolls in
his sleep. Beads of sweat clung to his forehead and
he'd managed to get all the laundry wrapped
around his arms and legs.

Everything was dark but by the light of a street
lamp outside the jam-jar walls, he could see Rubella
sleeping. There was a long line of drool running
down her cheek and forming a puddle on the
pillow.

'Bleeeccchhhhh!' said Neville quietly. He
couldn't share a bedroom with that great, snoring,
smelly carbuncle for another second. He had to
escape if it was the last thing he did.

He kicked off the dirty clothes and sat up. Being
brave and escaping was scary, but he had to get
back home.

'Think of Captain Brilliant,' Neville told himself. 'Just get up, walk to the door and think of Captain Brilliant.'

Rubella didn't stir as Neville sneaked across the cluttered room to the door. She didn't even shift when he stubbed his toe on a bent floorboard and had to cover his face with his hands to stop himself hopping about and shouting 'OW . . . OW . . . OOWWW!'

The door handle was at troll height and Neville could only reach it using a filthy dressing-gown that hung from a hook on the back of the door. He climbed it like a rope. 'Think of Captain Brilliant,' he told himself as he swung.

Neville climbed back down, poked his tongue out at Rubella and headed into the dark hallway.

In the darkness he could feel the rumble of Clod and Malaria snoring in their room at the other end of the landing. Neville wondered if he should leave a 'Thank You for Having Me' note for his troll parents, but then decided it wouldn't be a very good escape if he let them know he was going.

Neville couldn't wait to see the look on his mum and dad's faces when he got home. His escape would be so brave that the world would hail him as a superhero and his parents would grovel at his feet saying things like, 'Oh, son, how can we ever repay you?' and 'We're so, so proud of you, Super Neville. How lovely to have a hero in the family.'

Neville was enjoying the thought of being Super Neville so much that he didn't notice he had made it down the stairs and was now marching across the grimy kitchen with a big smile on his face. This bravery stuff was easier than it seemed. All he had to do was keep his chin held high, think of Captain Brilliant and . . .

'*Ggrrrrrrr . . . Ggrrrrrrrrrrrrrrrrr . . .*
GGRRRRRRRRRRR . . .'

Neville stopped dead on the spot, then very slowly turned round. There on the kitchen table,

poised and ready to pounce, was Rabies, the troll mole, teeth bared and slobbering angrily.

'N-n-nice, er, giant moley,' whimpered Neville. Captain Brilliant wasn't here now! 'G-go back to sleep n-now, Rabies,' he said. 'B-b-bedtime.'

Neville scanned the shadowy kitchen for something to distract Rabies. Broom handle? . . . No . . . Stack of newspapers? . . . No . . . Broken dish? . . . No . . . Discarded copy of the *Sunday Grimes*? . . . No . . . There had to be something.

'*GGRRRRRRRRRRRRR.*' Rabies hooked his claws over the end of the table and pounced, sailing through the air like a furry, black torpedo. Neville ducked then curled into a tiny ball. Rabies flew over him and landed with a thud on the kitchen floor, sending a stack of pans clattering in all directions.

Neville looked frantically for something, anything to stop Rabies from attacking him. Then suddenly he remembered . . .

'The rat patty!' Neville gasped. He plunged his hand inside his pyjama pocket and pulled out the greasy lump of meat, holding it high for Rabies to see.

Rabies stopped stalking. He sat on his haunches, tilted his head to one side and sniffed the air.

'Good Rabies,' Neville whispered. Rabies sniffed again. 'A nice stinky rat patty for the good moley.'

Rabies rolled over on to his back and wagged his little stump of a tail. He whined slightly, just like Napoleon used to when he wanted a doggy treat.

Neville threw the patty to Rabies, who snaffled it up in his jaws and scampered off to eat it, wagging his tail as he went.

Neville could have cried with relief. How many scares could one person cope with? At least, when he got home, he could tell his best friends Terrance and Archie about how he escaped from hideous trolls and warded off a fierce killer mole. He felt braver than he had ever felt before.

Neville headed for the green curtain. If he stayed low and ran quickly, all he had to do was follow the trail of lanterns back to the water pipe without being seen. He'd make it up the pipe somehow. *You can do this*, he thought and drew back the green curtain.

What Neville was expecting to see was the Bulches' yard and the pathway leading down Washing Machine Hill. Instead he saw a wrinkled old prune of a troll lady standing on the front step. She looked at him in horror. He looked back and screamed.

The last thing Neville remembered was hearing the words 'EEEEEEEEEKKKKKK! IT'S A BLIGHTER! A ROTSOME GONKER! EEEEEEKKKK!' as Gristle Pilchard brought her walking stick down on his head, with a mighty *WALLOP*.

Meanwhile

Pong stood on Neville's bed in a
shower of white feathers. He had
ripped all the pillows to shreds
and eaten the pillowcases.
They tasted of cotton and
sleep and spit.

'Ooooooorrrrhhhhh,' he
said. Then he burrowed into
the mountain of feathers and
curled up to sleep. In the
morning, he was going to peel
the wallpaper off the walls of
Marjorie and Herbert's bedroom.
That would be fun . . .

A Very Bad Headache

BAAAAAAAAAAAAANNNNNNNGGGGG! The ticker-dinger-thinger shook the house.

Neville woke up, wrapped snugly in a thick smelly blanket, lying across a pile of newspapers in the corner of the kitchen. His head felt like someone had screwed the top off, stuck in an egg-whisk and scrambled his brains. He reached up and felt a big, egg-sized bump beneath his hair.

'Ouch,' he said.

'Oh, you're back,' came Malaria's voice. 'What's your name again?' She was sitting at the kitchen table smoking her clay pipe alongside Clod and a rather angry-looking Mrs Pilchard.

'Neville,' said Neville, rubbing the bump. 'What's going on?'

'Oh, Neville, that's it. Well, Neville . . . you stirred up quite a rumpus,' said Malaria. 'You've been asleep for three bangs and three bongs straight.'

'Lazy lump,' Mrs Pilchard muttered under her breath.

'What happened?' asked Neville.

'Think you gave Mrs Pilchard a bit of a fright. She gave you a good clonk on the noggin,' said Clod. 'Ain't that right, Gristle?'

Gristle Pilchard was clinging to a mug of nettle tea with both hands like it was a life-ring in the middle of the ocean. She looked at Neville the same way someone would look at the bearded lady at a fun-fair. It was a mixture of fascination and utter disgust.

'Ahh yes, the gonker . . . There I was, minding my own business picking thistles on the hill to make some thorny-barb beer, when I hear all kinds of rambunkin' coming from your house. I took a peek through the curtain to see what in earth was occurinatin' and this grot jumps at me from the shadows. He attacked me.'

'I did not!' yelped Neville.

'He did,' Mrs Pilchard shouted. 'I thought I was a goner for sure!'

Neville sat up on his elbows. He felt wobbly and a bit sick.

'Belly, fetch your brother some stew. He looks a bit blurty if you ask me,' said Malaria.

Rubella was sitting at the far end of the table, staring at Neville like he was a dog poo she had just trodden in.

'Tell him to get it himself,' she snapped angrily.

Malaria blew a long puff of purple smoke from her nostrils and scowled. 'Do as you're told, young lady,' she said. 'Nev wouldn't be in this mess if you'd kept your beady peepers on him.'

Rubella stomped to the stove and fetched Neville a bowl of left sock stew. She plonked it down hard next to him on the floor.

'Don't choke,' she whispered. 'You lazy little bunion.'

Neville tried to be brave and stare back for as long as he could, but Rubella was too big and too frightening, so he took a sip of stew instead. It was stringy and got caught in his teeth but the cheesy flavour wasn't quite as bad as he had imagined.

'I'm sure Neville didn't mean to frighten you, eh, Nev?' said Malaria. Neville shook his head.

'Then what was he up to?' said Mrs Pilchard. 'If you ask me, he was causing trouble. That's all these overlings do. Cause trouble and make noise.'

'That's not true,' said Neville, wriggling out of the blanket. He might be afraid of Rubella but he wasn't going to let an old curmudgeon like Gristle Pilchard push him around. 'I was . . . I was just . . .' What could he say? He couldn't tell them he had been trying to run away from their horrid house and horrid town and horrid world. He wanted to go home, but he didn't want to upset them. 'I was just exploring,' he said.

'Ha!' Clod beamed. 'He's got Bulch spirit, ain't you, Nev? He's like his dooda.'

'You're not my dooda,' said Neville. Clod looked confused.

'See, Gristle,' said Malaria. 'He wasn't trying to hurt you.'

'Hmmm,' said Mrs Pilchard. 'He was trying to steal my . . . thistles. Admit it!'

'Eeuurrrgh,' said Neville. 'That is gross. I'd never try and steal your thistles.'

'Maybe he was, maybe he wasn't,' humphed Gristle. 'It doesn't solve the problem of what you're going to do about that lot.'

'What?' said Neville. 'What lot?'

Malaria pointed to the jam-jar wall behind him. 'Them,' she said.

Neville turned to look at the wall and jumped to his feet in surprise. On the other side of the jam jars was a gaggle of faces pressed against the glass, staring at him. *So much for escaping*, he thought.

'All the commotion three sleeps ago woke up half the street. Everyone is very curious,' said Clod.

'Word spreads fast down here. They've been queuing up for days to get a look at you,' Malaria joined in. 'You've become the talk of the town.'

Mrs Pilchard grunted and spat a mouthful of tea on to the floor. 'It's been a long time since we've had someone of the likes of you down in the underneath,' she said. 'Overlings are rare down here. That's why you gave me such a fright.'

Neville went to the table and climbed on to a barrel chair.

'You mean there've been others like me down here?' he said. 'Where are they? Can I talk to them?'

'No one remembers where they went,' said Clod. 'Us trolls aren't famous for our good memories. It's all a mystery.'

'One minute one of you overlings is down here with us,' said Mrs Pilchard. 'And the next, they're not.'

Neville breathed a sigh of relief. That meant that any other humans who came down to the underneath must have been able to escape. There was still hope for him yet.

WOO-WAAA-WOO-WAAA-WOO-WAAA . . .

Suddenly a siren echoed across the town from the ticker-dinger-thinger.

'Well,' said Malaria. 'That's unusual.'

'What's that sound?' asked Neville. 'I thought the ticker-dinger-thinger only went bong, bang and boom.'

'Well I never,' chuckled Clod. 'That, Nev, is the Trollabaloo alarm.'

'What's that?'

'What's a trollabaloo?' said Gristle Pilchard. 'The boy's got grunts for brains.'

'Sssshhh,' said Malaria. 'A trollabaloo is just what we need right now. Nev's still here for now and I say it's about time we show him off a bit. What d'ya say?'

'You mean . . .' said Clod.

'Indeedy,' said Malaria. 'It's time to meet the town, Neville my lump.'

'Is there going to be a party?' Neville asked. Malaria bent down so that her nose was almost against his.

'Just you wait, grub,' she said. 'A trollabaloo is the best kind of party there is under the whole wide world.' Then she did something that Neville wasn't expecting. She planted a big, wet kiss on his forehead. 'Just you wait.'

A Trollabaloo

Neville felt them all coming before he saw them. It started like a distant rumble, but before long the whole of Washing Machine Hill was shaking under the heavy *tromp-tromp-tromp* of even more trolls hurrying to the jam-jar house.

Through the kitchen wall he watched them marching up the path. There were hundreds of trolls coming from every direction.

'Here.' Malaria handed Neville a pair of Pong's tattered dungarees. They were made from bits of old handkerchief and bath towel. Neville threw his pyjamas into the corner and put the dungarees on.

'Hmmmm,' said Malaria, clicking her tongue. 'Not quite right. You have to look extra special for a trollabaloo.'

She scooped up a handful of dirt from the floor and rubbed it through Neville's hair, then moulded it into two little horns. 'Perfect,' she said.

'What d'ya think?'

Neville looked at himself in a broken mirror on the wall. 'I look a bit like . . . like one of you,' he said.

Through the jam-jar walls he watched as every troll man, woman and child assembled outside. They each had a blanket rolled up under their arm and were carrying heaps of food and baskets filled with all sorts of strange and wonderful-looking things.

Malaria told Neville to come into the yard and watch the preparations. 'There ain't nothing like a good trollabaloo to raise the spirits,' she said.

Neville ventured out through the green curtain but stayed close to the back of Malaria's legs. He had never seen so many trolls at the same time and it made his heart thump against his ribs.

From between Malaria's knees, Neville watched as all the blankets were laid on the ground, end to multicoloured end. Then all the elderly trolls (and there were lots of them) got down on their rickety

knees and produced big, scary-looking needles and
thick twine from their baskets and apron pockets.
They worked fast and furiously, sewing the edges of
all the blankets together with enormous stitches and
knots. Neville's mouth hung open in delight. Soon,
the entire hill disappeared beneath a brightly
coloured patchwork blanket that spread all the way
down to the streets below.

Next, the child trolls spread out plates of food

and jugs brimming with exotic-looking drinks all over the new soft covering of the hill while the adults lit hundreds of milk-bottle lanterns and strung them up from long poles.

'How's about that?' asked Malaria with a big smile on her face. 'Perfect party spot if ever I saw one.'

'It's . . . it's lovely,' said Neville, and this time he wasn't lying.

Clod appeared at the green curtain and stepped outside. He was dressed in a ragged black suit that was ten sizes too small for him, with no shirt on underneath and bare feet. 'Oh, Clod, you look squibbly,' said Malaria. 'Absolutely honksome.'

'Hello, my bottom blossom,' said Clod, kissing Malaria on the cheek. 'Hello, Nev,' he said to Neville. 'How you enjoying all the getting ready?'

'It looks . . . squibbly?' said Neville, not quite sure how to describe what he was looking at.

'That it does, Nev, that it does.'

Clod marched into the middle of the busy crowd and raised his hands in the air. 'FRIENDS, GUESTS AND VISITROLLS!' he yelled over the hubbub. 'MY LOVELY WIFELING AND ME HAVE SOMEONE WE THINK YOU SHOULD MEET!' All the trolls whooped and hollered.

'HE AIN'T BEEN 'ERE LONG, BUT I'D SAY IT'S ABOUT TIME YOU SAID 'ELLO TO NEVILLE BULCH!'

With that, a band of bizarre bagpipers struck up a lively jig and the trollabaloo leapt into action. Malaria took Neville's hand in her great stumpy fingers and led him into the crowd.

Neville tugged on Malaria's arm. 'My name isn't Neville Bulch, it's Neville Brisket,' he said.

'Codswallop,' said Malaria. 'You're a Bulch now.'

'Neville Bulch.' Neville tried out his new name with a gulp.

'You're one of us now,' Malaria said. 'I'm your mooma and Clod's your dooda and Rubella's your . . .'

'Sister!' Neville gasped. He wanted to run away and hide and protect his bumpy head. He didn't want to be Rubella's brother. He glanced at her through the crowd. She was standing with Gruntilda and Thicket, and she was glaring at him.

'Come on, Nev,' said Clod, pulling him off through the crowd. 'Lots of trolls to meet.'

Children ran over to say hello to Neville and invited him to join in their games of Hunt the

Foozle and Pin the Sting on the Slurch, a scary-looking beast with hideous teeth like screwdrivers. But, for now, he was happy watching from a distance.

Clod introduced Neville to Flotsam and Limpet Mossgrot, the twins from the baked bean can house a little further down the hill. They said Neville could come round if he wanted and told him they'd show him how to play badgerball. Neville was still a little nervous, but one thing was for sure. It felt nice to be popular for a change. Though he wasn't sure about badgerball.

The singing and dancing continued long into the evening. There were slow dances and fast jigs and twisty twirlers and slidey salsas. There were songs and stories and chase games. Even Gristle Pilchard joined in.

Everyone was beaming and brimming and briny with fun. After a while, Neville forgot about the bump on his head and found the courage to stray a little way from Clod and Malaria's side. He said hello to one or two of the less scary-looking neighbours and, though he wasn't sure, he thought he might be having fun.

The only person not having fun at the trollabaloo was Rubella. She sat on a cushion near the front doorway of the house and tugged at the hideous pink dress Malaria had forced her to wear. She was fuming with rage. All night, Gruntilda had been pointing and laughing at the puffy, pink monstrosity and, even worse, Thicket had laughed too. The thorniest guy around was laughing at her and all because of Neville.

She stared at her new brother through narrowed, sulky eyes and devised a plan. She'd get rid of the squirmy little squealer if it was the last thing she did.

Meanwhile

Herbert stood frozen to the spot with a look of utter bewilderment on his face. He scratched his head. How on earth had the lawnmower ended up on the dining room table?

Pong snickered. He knew exactly how it had got there.

Rubella's Plan

'Psssssst.' Rubella jabbed a finger into Neville's side. 'Wake up, you dungle.'

Neville stirred from a far-off dream and rubbed his eyes. It was extremely late and all the partying of the trollabaloo had left him exhausted. Rubella's room was silent and very, very dark. He had been in a deep sleep and the last person he wanted to see at this horrid hour was Whale Waist herself.

'Mooma told me to take you home,' she whispered.

'I am,' said Neville, still half asleep.

'No, you grot brain, your real home. Back up top.'

Neville sat up. Home! Comfy bed and good food and sun and baths and . . .

'Why are you helping me?' he asked.

'Mooma said she didn't want you any more,' Rubella lied. 'And Dooda too.'

'Oh,' said Neville. 'Why?'

91

'They just said they were bored of you, so they wanted me to take you back and get Pong.'

Neville couldn't help but feel a little upset. 'But the pipes won't stretch,' he remembered.

'I know another way,' said Rubella. 'Much quicker than the pipes. Let's go. There isn't much time before the bang.'

Neville wriggled out from under the blanket. Rubella had already gone out through the green curtain and he had to run to catch up to her.

'Shouldn't I say goodbye first?' asked Neville as they started down the hill.

'Naaaaaaah,' said Rubella, shrugging her shoulders. 'I don't think they really care. They thought you were a slimy, squirming, crying wimp.'

Rubella didn't say anything to Neville after that. She didn't have to. The trollabaloo had been brilliant, and now Mooma and Dooda didn't want him. Tears started to roll quietly down Neville's cheeks.

As they walked, Neville looked at the blanket floor beneath their feet. There would be a big reverse trollabaloo in the morning when everyone came to unpick the stitches and he was going to miss it. He would have loved to watch how quickly the trolls could work, taking down the lanterns and snipping and pulling all the twine.

'Never mind,' he told himself. 'I don't belong here anyway. What do I care if some ugly, smelly trolls don't want me?'

The Bog of the Slurches

'I think we're lost,' said Neville. He remembered passing through the big stone gate and taking the lantern tunnels when he came into the town. Rubella had led him somewhere completely different and the way up ahead was getting steeper and narrower.

'Nope,' said Rubella, as she plodded on ahead. 'This is right. It's a short cut.'

On they went, up and up until the cliff wall at their side vanished and they came to the beginning of a big swamp that stretched through a rocky canyon. There was gloopy, bubbling mud on the ground and weird, spindly trees that looked like upside-down spiders on sticks. Neville stopped in his tracks when he saw that Rubella was heading straight for it.

'I don't want to go through there,' he said. Rubella turned round and scowled at him.

'Well, you have to,' she said. 'It's the only way home.'

'I . . . I . . . don't want to. I'll just wait till the next grab night.'

The bog looked like something from a horror movie he had seen at Archie's house when Archie's parents were out. It was very big, very wet and very, very dark.

'I don't care if you don't want to, you spit stain,' Rubella barked. 'It's the only way up, there's no other way out of the underneath and you can't stay here. No one wants you.'

She grabbed Neville by the arm and pushed him forward.

'Not long now,' she said with a spiteful grin.

Neville tumbled headfirst into the sticky ooze at the edge of the bog. It was hot and smelled of rotten dead things.

'Eeeuuuurrrrrrgggghhhhh,' he gasped, clambering back to his feet, dripping in brown swamp water. The mucky stuff was already up to his waist and he was only a tiny way from the edge of the swamp where Rubella stood.

'Go on,' she said. 'Wade out a little way and

you'll see the pipe. It'll lead you straight home.'

Neville turned and peered into the misty darkness.

'I can't see it,' he said. 'Are you sure this is right?'

'Absolutely,' said Rubella. 'Just a bit further and you'll see it.'

Neville waded out slowly towards the centre of the bog. It was tiring work. The mud was thick and clung to his arms and legs as he moved. *I hope there're no crocodiles in here*, he thought to himself. *Please, please, please no crocodiles.*

'I still can't see anything,' he called back to Rubella. 'I think you made a mistake.'

Then something caught his eye. It was a wooden sign, nailed to a long pole sticking out of the bog. Now, even Neville wasn't 'fraidy enough to be scared of just a wooden sign on its own. It was what was written on it that scared him.

In big red letters, the sign said 'BEWARE! SLURCHES!'

Slurches? Why did that sound so familiar? Neville racked his brain and tried to remember where he'd heard the name 'Slurch' before. Whatever they were, there wouldn't be a 'beware'

sign if they were friendly.

'Keep going,' Rubella called again from the swamp edge. 'You're almost there.'

Neville was about to call and say he was coming back to dry land when he suddenly remembered exactly where he'd heard 'Slurch' before. It was the game at last night's trollabaloo. The other troll children had invited him to play Pin the Sting on the Slurch.

His lower lip began to tremble. He remembered the picture painted on an old bed sheet. The slurch was a jet black, massively long worm with row upon row of gnashing teeth like screwdrivers, and a big pointy sting.

Neville froze in the mud. Rubella had brought him right into the bog of the slurches. She wasn't trying to help him get home. She was trying to get him eaten. He whimpered. Too afraid to run back and too afraid to go forward, he froze.

What Neville didn't know was that, while he was desperately trying to decide what to do, an enormous slurch had already slimed and slithered its way out of the depths in front of him and was sniffing hungrily at his ankles below the water. It

was about to take its first bite of sinewy overling
flesh when it caught a whiff of something else.
Something far more appealing.

Somewhere nearby, the slurch could smell the
unmistakable stink of a fat troll girl. Trolls were far
tastier than whatever the twigling was that stood in
the bog. The slurch slugged its way towards the
swamp bank and slurped a giggle to itself, thinking
how lovely it would be to chomp on the juicy
porklet. It could spend hours picking at her bones
and savouring every little scrap of the great chubby
chunkling.

'Don't stop, snotbag!' Rubella was practically
jumping up and down with anger. 'Keep going.' She
didn't understand. Normally, a slurch would have
gobbled up anyone who had waded into the mud by
now. 'Keep going,' she yelled again. 'KEEP GO–
AAAAAAAAAAAAGGGGHHHHHH!'

Rubella screamed as a black wormlike tail shot
out of the stinking water and coiled around her
ankle. It yanked her high into the air until she was
hanging upside-down like a pig in a butcher's shop.

Neville spun round. Rubella wriggled in mid-air,
flapping her arms and legs.

'Save me!' she screamed. 'Save me!'

Neville didn't know what to do. He was terrified. The slurch's head rose up out of the swamp and flashed its screwdriver teeth at the hollering girl. It was terrible to behold. The slurch was even worse than the painting at the party. Neville hated Rubella. She was spiteful and cruel and made him believe his mooma and dooda didn't want him AND SHE'D TRIED TO GET HIM EATEN! But he couldn't stand by and watch as Rubella was ground up into mincemeat by all those teeth. He wanted to – the fat gonk deserved everything she got – but he couldn't.

Oh no . . . was this it? There had been a million times already that Neville had thought might be 'it', but this really WAS it . . .

Neville was going to have to be brave. He closed his eyes, thought of Captain Brilliant in his green pants and grabbed the Beware sign with both hands.

At first it didn't want to budge, and his fingers were wet and slimy against the wooden pole. Neville pulled and yanked until, with a satisfying *sllluuurrrpppppppp*, the sign came free from the mud.

'I'll save you, Rubella,' he yelled, slopping back towards shore and the thrashing slurch as fast as he could. As he battled through the mud, Neville sang the Captain Brilliant theme tune at the top of his voice to give him extra courage.

'CAPTAIN BRILLIANT
THERE'S NO ONE MORE RESILIENT
ALWAYS SAVES THE SCENE
IN HIS PANTS OF GREEN . . .'

'Help! Help!' Rubella yelled from above. The slurch lunged for one of her chubby arms as she flailed around. Its teeth clashed together in a dreadful scrape of metal. It missed by a hair's breadth and Rubella punched it on the nose. 'STOP SINGING AND DO SOMETHING!' she screamed.

Neville reached the slurch and started jabbing at it with the pointy end of the signpost. It didn't seem to be working. He wasn't strong enough to do any real damage and the slurch was far too interested in eating Rubella to care about a small boy with a signpost.

Next, Neville tried to whack at the slurch with the flat sign itself. He beat at the creature's slimy flesh as hard as he could. That seemed to work. The slurch coiled away from the blows and turned its head away from the troll to loom at Neville with hundreds of bright green eyes.

Neville hit it again, harder this time, and sang at the top of his lungs. 'DA-DA-DOO . . . HIS PANTS GO FLASH!'

'BBBPPLLLLUUUUHHHHHRRRRGGG!' yowled the slurch.

'Let her go,' Neville shouted. 'Let her go.'

He whacked the slurch again, and again . . . and again. It didn't seem to be working.

'BA-BA-BOO . . . THE BAD GUY'S
THRASHED!'

The slurch wriggled and twisted and yowled
again. Neville gasped. It was his singing. The slurch
hated the sound. It moaned and screeched and
shook its head.

'GO CAPTAIN GO-GO!' Neville sang. 'GO-
GO-GO!'

The slurch dropped Belly into the water with a
mighty sploosh. No sooner had she poked her head
out of the swamp water, she screamed, 'RUN!' and
scrabbled back up on to the swamp bank.

Neville dropped the sign into the mud and
followed her while the slurch twisted and splashed
with anger. It wouldn't be long before it was back in
pursuit of them both. Neville had to think quickly.

They were only just in time. The slurch rose back
out of the swamp and charged towards Neville. Its
eyes flashed red and yellow in furious rage and its
teeth clanged together like dustbin lids.

'SING!' Neville shouted.

'WHAT?' Rubella shouted back.

'JUST DO IT!'

Neville flung his arms wide and sang as loudly as

he could. The slurch wheezed and spluttered like it was going to be sick.

'SING, RUBELLA!' Neville yelled.

Rubella let rip a great high-pitched note and the slurch tumbled backwards.

'What's happening?' asked Rubella between breaths.

'It's not a music fan,' said Neville.

The slurch started squirming and slapping its tail, straining its head this way and that.

'OOOOOOO-EEEEEEEE-OOOOOO!' sang Rubella.

'PANTS OF GREEN!' sang Neville.

'BRUUUURRRRGGG!' howled the slurch, before sinking back into the swamp with one final disgusting, oozy plop.

Rubella looked at Neville in amazement.

'You did it,' she said with wide eyes. Her voice was barely a whisper.

Better Than
Captain Brilliant

'Where've you been?' said Clod. 'I've been worrying my barnacles off, I have.'

Rubella looked at Neville. When the Mooma and Dooda found out that she had tried to get him eaten by slurches, they'd ground her for the next five hundred bangs.

'We . . . well . . . um,' she said.

'Out with it, young lady,' said Malaria, folding her arms angrily.

'We got into a bit of trouble,' said Rubella. 'At the Slurches' Bog.'

'You took Neville up there?' asked Clod. 'There's nowhere more dangerous in all of the underneath. What in earth were you thinking?'

Rubella looked at her feet. She started to cry.

'I asked her to show me,' said Neville. Rubella

looked at him in surprise. 'I asked Rubella to show me the slurches and she took me because she wanted to do something nice for me.'

'That don't sound like you, Belly,' said Malaria. 'You feeling all right?'

Rubella nodded, looked at Neville who smiled, then she nodded again.

'Neville saved me,' she said. 'I got grabbed by a big 'un and Neville saved me.'

''S'at true, Nev?' asked Clod. 'Don't sound much like you neither.'

Neville shrugged.

'Well, you're a blunkin' hero,' beamed Malaria. She rushed forward and scooped Neville up in her big arms.

A hero. Neville a hero? He . . . he . . . he had never, in his whole life, ever been called a hero. He could feel a warm feeling filling him up from the bottom of his toes to the top of his head.

'I think we should head out for a day on the town,' said Clod. 'To celebrate having a hero in the family.'

'What do you think, hero?' asked Malaria.

'I'd like that,' said Neville. He could barely contain his enormous smile.

As Malaria carried him out of the door, Neville glanced back at Rubella. She was scowling.

'Come on . . . sis,' said Neville.

'You tell anyone I was scared and you're dead,' said Rubella. 'And don't call me sis.'

Meanwhile

CRRRRAAAAAASSSSSSHHHHH!!!!

'Oooooorrrrrrrrrrrrrrrhhhhhhhhhhhhh!'

SSSHHHHAAAATTTTTTTEEEEERRRRR!!!

'Mmmmmmmmmmmm.'

TTTTTTHHHHHUUUUUDDDD!!!

'Don't do that, Neville.'

CCRRUUUUUUUNNCCHH . . .

CCRRUUUUUUUNNCCHH . . .

CCRRUUUUUUUNNCCHH . . .

'Neville, I'm warning you.'

CRASH!!!!!!

'NEVILLE!'

A Squibbly Day Out

Neville felt brave and daring as he rode on Malaria's back down Washing Machine Hill and into the centre of town.

He waved at other trolls as they passed, retold his story of defeating a slurch to a group of gossiping grannies and even got to hold Rabies' lead.

Clod showed Neville the statue of Lady Jaundice the 'Troll That Stole', and the tower where Sir Arthritis III had one of his heads chopped off. Rubella showed him how to jump on cockroaches and make them go *crunch*.

They heard a band playing strange instruments called priddles that were like fiddles but with almost a hundred strings. The sound was like a million cats wailing at once. Neville kept his fingers in his ears but he liked watching the priddlers play.

After a snack of moss cakes from Thistle Twollop's cake stand, Clod swapped some tin cans

for a fishing pole
and a net for
Neville. He
spent the
undernoon
showing Neville
how to catch eels

from the sludge puddles.

At dinnertime, they ate at Alopecia Grubber's
famous restaurant. Neville ordered slices of dried
centipede and a mushroom salad freshly harvested
from Alopecia's shoulders. The centipede tasted
bitter and crunchy but the mushrooms were warm,
fluffy and tasty so Neville didn't mind too much. He
threw anything he didn't like to Rabies who was
waiting under his chair for treats.

When they'd finished licking all the plates and
bowls clean, Clod and
Malaria took Neville
to the theatre.
They watched an
exciting play
about a kind and
gentle ogre that

lived in a castle at the top of a beanstalk. He and his ogre wife were happy spending their days baking ear-wax brownies until the evil overling 'Jack' slithered up the beanstalk and stole everything from under the ogres' noses.

Neville watched with wide eyes. He had never heard this version of the story before.

All the trolls in the theatre booed and hissed whenever the actor playing Jack came on stage. He wore a scary human mask and had blood running from the corners of his twisted mouth.

'BOOOOOOOO! HISSSSSS! BOOOOOO!' Before he knew it, Neville was booing the overling along with all the trolls. Especially when the cruel thing cut down the beanstalk while the ogre was climbing down it to give a basket of ear-wax brownies to Jack and his murderous mother. Neville thought for a moment as the actor trolls all bowed. Who knew that overlings could be so . . . so . . . monstrous?

Changeling

Neville often thought about the scary and evil Jack from the theatre show as he rode around on Clod's shoulders or helped Malaria in the kitchen. But, as bang followed bong followed bang followed bong, something strange started happening. The more Neville thought about Jack, the more he couldn't quite remember why he seemed so familiar.

In the evenings he stopped worrying about troll food and always ate whatever Malaria made for dinner. He stopped finding even the strangest foods disgusting. He found he liked battered badger the best.

At night, Neville would curl up in Rubella's laundry pile and practise making faces at the ceiling or flicking bogeys at passing fireflies.

One night while he lay dozing, he felt something unexpected on his left shoulder. It was a kind of soft, round lump. He tried to pull it off but realized

113

it was attached to him.

He very quietly got up and skittered across the room to the broken mirror. There, in the darkness, he could see the round top of a toadstool sticking up out of the corner of his shoulder and neck. He touched it carefully. It sent a shiver all the way down his spine.

He was about to skitter back to the laundry pile when his foot scuffed against something in the dark. It was an old boot, lying on its side. Neville picked it up and, without even thinking about it, took a big bite. The boot tasted like pond water and leather and overlings. He recognized the strangely familiar scent and it excited him immensely. He turned back to the mirror.

'Ooooooooorrrrrrhhhhhhhh,' Neville said to his grey-green reflection.

Meanwhile

Ka-lump ka-lump ka-lump!

Pong tore through the house with a pair of
Marjorie's high-heeled shoes on his feet.

Ka-lump ka-lump!

Overlings were so much fun. He kicked a
stumpy leg and laughed with delight as the
shoe shot from his foot
and wedged, heel first,
into the living-room
wall. Brilliant!

Grab Night

BOOM!!!!

The whole town shook. Clod jumped up from the breakfast table and ran to the green curtain.

'It's the ticker-dinger-thinger,' he yelled. Outside, Neville heard trolls shouting and whooping. 'Grab Night . . . Grab Night . . . Grab Night!'

Grab night! Neville knew he had been waiting for this. But he couldn't remember why. His whole body tingled with excitement.

'About blunkin' time,' said Malaria. 'We're running low on left socks.' She grabbed the broom handle and banged on the ceiling. 'Belly, get down here. It's grab night tonight. We should all go to show Nev how it's done.'

'I'M NOT DEAF!' screamed Rubella. 'AND I'M NOT COMING.'

'YOU MARCH YOUR LUMPY RUMP DOWN 'ERE THIS INSTANT, YOUNG LADY.

We're out of things to chew, and we need all hands on deck,' Malaria screamed back.

Rubella stuck her hand through the hole in the ceiling and flicked a giant bogey at her mooma. 'NOOOOOOOOO!!'

'THAT'S IT!' Malaria hurled the broom handle across the room and stormed up the stairs. Neville sat and listened to the shrieks, screams and thuds coming from above.

Clod smiled at Neville from across the room and rolled his eyes. Neville giggled.

'Who'll win, d'ya reckon?' wondered Clod. Neville shrugged and listened to more clattering and banging.

After what seemed like an awfully long time, there came the sound of Rubella's door opening and heavy footsteps clomping down the stairs. Malaria appeared at the bottom of them looking dishevelled and dazed. She had a sock caught in her hair and there was an unravelled toilet roll wrapped round her feet.

'Belly ain't comin',' she said sheepishly.

Pipes

It was time for the grab.

After a dinner of fish and boiled weasel, Clod and Malaria led Neville high up into the tunnels. They passed along stone passageways and through dank sewer pipes that Neville had not seen since the night he first came underneath. Although strangely he didn't remember it at all.

'This might be a bit of a struggle for you, the first time,' said Clod. 'You knows I got myself into a right pickled mess, the first time I tried to squeeze through the toilet.'

'Don't you go scaring him,' said Malaria. 'You'll be fine, my pook. Just hold your breath and think of slippery things, I find that does the trick.'

Neville had forgotten what it was like to be scared. Instead he felt excited at the thought of squishing through those tiny pipes and exploring the world up above. After all, he'd never been before . . . had he?

The three turned into a tunnel whose ceiling was covered in hundreds of tiny lanterns. Neville cooed to himself as he saw an enormous painting on the wall. In it, he could see trolls of all ages and sizes, and they were building the town. There were lady trolls weaving baskets and men trolls stacking rocks and rubbish to build houses. He could even see young trolls boiling pots of toadstool tonic. And at the very top of the picture there was a troll reaching up out of a toilet and shaking hands with an overling.

'What does it mean?' asked Neville.

'Dunno,' said Clod. 'No one remembers.'

Neville looked at the strange pink-skinned thing on the other side of the toilet. 'I don't like those overlings,' he said. 'Although I'd like to see one.'

Neville thought about what he had just said. Something was wrong but he couldn't put his finger on it.

'Well, youngling,' said Clod. 'Tonight you can go see as many snoring overlings as you like.'

Neville giggled but it came out like a little growl. 'I can't wait,' he said.

'Not far now, my lump,' said Malaria as they rounded the corner into an enormous chamber filled with trolls. It looked as if the entire town had turned up for the grab tonight. There were hundreds of trolls and they were all gathering near the pipes that covered the walls like the holes in Swiss cheese.

'This bit's really weird,' Clod whispered in Neville's ear. He pointed to Glottel Potch, the mayor of the town, as he marched proudly into the centre of the chamber. He cleared his throat and everyone fell silent.

'My fellow underlings,' he shouted. 'Good

fortune, junk hunters. Bring back jubbly treasures.' Then he sang a long low note at the top of his voice. The note was deep and rich and vibrated the floor and ceiling. Neville could feel it jittering his bones.

Then, more and more trolls joined in. They sang many different notes that together made a huge cacophony of singing. The walls began to shake and the pipes started glowing a bright, vibrant yellow.

Malaria bent down. 'That's troll magic,' she whispered to Neville.

Suddenly the singing stopped.

'GOOD FORTUNE, JUNK HUNTERS!' Glottel Potch shouted again.

Neville watched in amazement as each troll squished himself into the tiny openings. Even the tiniest of holes stretched like elastic and then returned to its normal size once the troll had slipped through.

'Troll magic,' said Clod with a wink. 'Our pipe is over here.'

They took Neville over to a teeny opening, no bigger than a chocolate biscuit. Above it was a little sign that said 'PIPE NUMBER 2674. CLOD, MALARIA, RUBELLA AND ~~PONG~~ NEVILLE BULCH'.

'Who's Pong?' asked Neville.

Clod and Malaria looked at each other. They looked confused, as if they had suddenly forgotten something. 'Not sure,' they said.

'But . . .' said Neville. The name Pong seemed familiar.

Before he could continue, Clod interrupted. 'Right, I'll go first, then you can follow me,' he said. 'Remember to think slippery thoughts and the troll magic will do the rest.'

Clod squeezed his arms, then his head and shoulders into the pipe. Neville gasped to see the metal stretch like a rubber band as his dooda vanished inside. In no time the only thing left of Clod were his chubby grey-green feet wriggling up inside the pipe.

'Fun, ain't it?' said Malaria.

'Lummy,' said Neville.

'Well then, lump,' she said. 'It's your turn. Ready?'

Neville stepped up to the pipe and touched the edge of it with a grubby finger. It twitched as if it were alive. He wasn't sure about this. It looked dark and scary and slimy.

Malaria put her hand on his shoulder. 'I'll be right behind you,' she said.

Neville took a deep breath, stepped back for a bit of a run-up, then launched himself at the pipe as Malaria whooped with pride.

'HERE WE GO!' he screamed as he ran.

There was a loud stretchy, creaking noise and Neville shot into the pipe like a bullet speeding through the barrel of an old rifle. He was twisted and shaken and spun and wobbled as he sped through the darkness. And then, with a great whoosh of water, Neville flew out of the toilet straight into Clod's arms.

'There you are,' Clod whispered. 'I was wondering where you'd got to.'

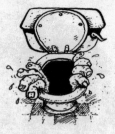

The Grab

Seconds after Neville came out of the toilet, Malaria whooshed through and landed next to him with a splash. The room was dark and everything was quiet.

'First,' said Clod, 'you have to sniff the air.'

The three of them sniffed.

'Then you have to listen and make sure the coast is clear,' said Malaria.

Neville strained his ears and sniffed again. 'Nothing,' he said.

'Let's go,' said Clod.

'Don't forget,' said Malaria, 'grab what you like but get as many left socks as you can.'

Neville nodded. He could feel the tingle of adventure in his belly again.

Clod headed out into the hallway and down the stairs. He wanted to rifle through the basement for fishing rods and building tools. Malaria headed for the airing cupboard to look for sheets and towels to make new dresses.

Neville crept to the bathroom door and peeked out. The hallway was inky black, but as his eyes were used to darkness he could see perfectly. There was something very familiar about this place. Like something from a dream he couldn't quite remember.

He passed his mooma in the dark, humming to herself as she rifled through the first door on the landing, and headed to the second door. Something about that door smelled inviting. The tingle of adventure was joined by another, prickly feeling. It was the feeling he had been here before.

He turned the handle and pushed. The door swung open to reveal a bedroom. The lights were off and everything was dark, but Neville could easily see two figures sleeping in a bright pink bed. Something felt so familiar. He wanted to cry and laugh and run away and he had no idea why. Was there something he had forgotten?

He crept on to the end of the bed and stalked towards the sleeping faces. Who were these overlings? Neville was about to lick the end of the lady overling's nose when the door burst open and a small grey-green thing bounded into the room burbling and cooing in excitement at the strange people in the house.

'BLLLLLUUUUUURRRRRRGGGGGG!' it yelled and threw a half-eaten frozen pizza across the room. Neville jumped from the bed and darted into the shadows.

'BRRRRRROOOOOOOOOOOOOHHHHH!' yelled the thing again.

'What the –?' snorted Herbert Brisket, waking with a start. He sat up in bed and switched on the bedside lamp. Pong had already galumphed back out of the door and down the hallway to find more things to throw, but Neville was now trapped against the back wall of the bedroom and in full view. Herbert saw the grubby thing with mud horns and screamed like a girl.

'Herbert,' snapped Marjorie. 'What on earth is wrong with you? Are you crazy?'

Herbert pointed to the far corner with bulging eyes and a drooping jaw. Marjorie flicked on her own bedside light to get a better look and peered straight at Neville. The muddy child crept forward

and stared back. He knew her face and it filled him with fear. Neville screamed. Then Marjorie screamed. She flew out of the bed, grabbed an umbrella from the corner and ran at him.

'Get out, you little beast,' she yelled. 'AAAAGGGHHH!'

She started swatting the air above his head like a crazed woman in a swarm of bees. Neville was about to make a dash for the door when, *THUD THUD THUD THUD*, Malaria ran into the bedroom.

'GET AWAY FROM MY SON!' she roared.

Surprise

Malaria looked like a dragon in the doorway.
She had been puffing on her pipe and smoke
swirled from her mouth and nostrils as she glowered
at Marjorie.

Marjorie screeched like a strangled turkey and
clambered over the bed towards Herbert who stood
gawping in disbelief.

Thud . . . THUD . . . THUD . . . Clod ran into the
bedroom.

'What's occurinatin', my lump?' he said.

Marjorie screeched even louder. Her face started
turning purple. Clod almost jumped out of his skin
at the odd little woman, wailing and babbling.

'Ssshhhhhh,' he said. 'You'll burst my barnacles.'

Marjorie started flapping her arms and
hopping from foot to foot. Then she let loose a
sound that would have shattered glass. Everyone
covered their ears.

'I think she's trying to scramble our brains,' shouted Clod over the din.

'Shut her up,' yelled Neville.

Malaria stomped forward and clamped her hand over Marjorie's mouth. 'Stop your gibbering,' she growled.

Marjorie wriggled free of Malaria's grip, grabbed Herbert who was still gawping silently and ran into the corner, brandishing the umbrella like a sword.

'Get out of my house,' she screamed. 'Get out, get out, GET OUT!'

'Give us your left socks,' shouted Clod.

Marjorie's eyes widened.

'What?' she said.

'Erm . . . give us your left socks and we'll leave,' said Clod.

'Socks?' said Marjorie. 'You monsters break into my house, ruin my sleep and scare the brains out of my husband . . . AND IT'S ALL FOR SOCKS?'

'Left socks,' said Malaria.

Marjorie turned from scared to angry. 'AAAAAAAAAAAAAGGGGHHHHHHH!' she screamed. She ran at Neville and started swatting at his head with the umbrella.

Malaria picked the woman off the floor and lifted her up level with her face.

'Don't you ever touch my son,' she growled.

Suddenly . . . *THUD THUD THUD THUD . . .* dripping with toilet water, Rubella appeared at the bedroom door and stomped into the room. Marjorie screamed again.

'THAT STINKING LITTLE WHELP AIN'T YOUR SON!' Rubella screamed, pointing a finger at Neville.

Everybody froze. All eyes were on Rubella.

'I remembered . . . He's nothing but a grubbly little overling. He might have grown a toadstool or two but he ain't one of us.'

And in a flash, Neville remembered. Flicking before his eyes, he saw Napoleon in the washing basket, the toilet, the grey-green hand, the tunnel, the lanterns, the town. He felt the fear that gripped him on the night he was snatched. He felt sick.

'WAIT!' Neville yelled. He stepped out of the shadows. 'She's right. M-M-Mum?'

Everyone froze again. All eyes were now on Neville.

'Mooma, not Mum,' said Malaria.

'No,' said Neville, pointing at Marjorie. 'Mum.'

'I'm not your mother,' said Marjorie. Malaria put Marjorie down and brushed herself off.

'What's going on, Nev?' asked Clod.

Neville edged nervously towards Marjorie. 'Mum, it's me . . . it's Neville.'

'You can't be,' said Marjorie. 'You're over there.' She pointed to the squat figure standing in the doorway and then she looked closely at Pong for the first time. She screamed like never before.

Neville ran forward and put his hand over his mum's mouth.

'I had forgotten,' he said. He turned to Clod and Malaria. 'Do you remember when I came to live with you?' he asked them.

'What d'ya mean?' said Malaria. 'You've always lived with us.'

'What's gotten into you, Nev?' asked Clod. 'You're a troll.'

Neville picked up a glass of water from the bedside table and poured it over his head. The mud ran away to reveal his overling face.

133

'Errr,' said Rubella, pulling a face. 'I think I'm going to be sick.'

'Try to remember,' Neville said. 'You grabbed me by accident. You thought I was Pong.'

'Pong?' said Malaria. The name clearly rang a bell. 'PONG!' She spun round and grabbed up the little troll who was chewing on a table leg. Its skin was a lot less grey-green than it used to be and a lot more rosy coloured. A horn had vanished from the side of his head and his teeth seemed straighter. 'Oh, my Pong, I'd forgotten all about you.'

Clod sprang to Malaria's side as he also
remembered. Rubella rolled her eyes and stuck out
her tongue, but even she looked pleased to see Pong.

Marjorie grabbed Herbert and shook his arm.
'Herbert,' she yelped. 'Look, it's Neville. We've
had a dirty changeling all along.' They both
stared at him. Neither of them approached him.

'I'm sorry,' said Marjorie. She shuffled forwards
then did something Neville was sure she had never
done before, ever. She bent down and hugged him
to her chest. It was a long, warm, proper 'mum' hug

and it warmed Neville all over. 'I'm so sorry.'

The two families stood hugging on either side of the bedroom for a long time.

'We need to be getting underneath soon,' said Clod as a large troll-sized tear ran down his face. 'You comin', Nev? There's room for you and Pong.'

Neville looked at his mooma and dooda and then at his mum and dad. He shook his head. 'I can't,' he said. 'I belong here.'

'Too right,' said Rubella.

Malaria blurted out a loud sob. 'You were such a jubbly troll,' she said. She put Pong down and gave Neville a wet kiss on the top of his head. 'We won't forget you.'

'I will,' said Rubella and stomped out of the door.

No one said anything else. Clod and Malaria shuffled back towards the bathroom with Pong. Neville just hugged his mum and dad, and listened to the sound of the toilet flushing and his troll family vanishing underneath.

'I won't forget you,' he whispered. 'Not even Rubella.'

One Last Thing

It was late at night and Neville couldn't sleep. He'd done his homework, packed his PE kit for tomorrow, brushed his teeth and washed his face, but something still wasn't right. His belly was grumbling with hunger but Neville couldn't think why. He had eaten all his dinner and polished off a bowl of ice cream. Something was missing.

He crept out of bed and out of his room. The laundry basket stood squat and overflowing in the corner by the bathroom.

In no time at all he was snacking on the tastiest left sock he had ever eaten.

'Oooooooorrrrrrrrrrrrhhhhh,' he said to himself. 'Lummy!'

Some Funly Thingies

Just in case you ever bump
into a troll wiffling his
way up your toilet, here're a
few words you can use for a
good ole' chattywag.

Accusatin'	Accusing
Blurty	Ill or sick
Brandyburp	A name for someone sweet and lovely
Chubbling	A great big fatty
Chunkling	An even bigger fatty
Dooda	A troll dad
Dooky	Dank and damp
Dungle	A big, slow, stupid beast

Dungle droppings	The poo of a dungle (yuck!)
Foozle	Like a dungle but a bit less smelly
Good gracicles	Goodness gracious!
Gonker	A criminal or bad guy
Grotsome	Cool
Grumptious	Gorgeous
Hinkapoot	A small, skittery animal
Honksome	Handsome
Hump-honker	A very happy person
Lummy	Yummy
Minch	More than a centimetre, less than an inch
Mooma	A troll mum
Nogginknocker	A fool or stupid person

Occurinatin'	Happening
Overling	A human
Pluglet	A baby
Rambunking	Naughty
Rotsome	Terrible or horrible
Slurch	A giant worm with teeth like screwdrivers
Squibbly	Lovely, great or wonderful
Starvatious	Starving
Trollabaloo	The best kind of party there is
Tummy-tinkler	A delicious delicacy
Underling	A troll
Wiffle	Sneak
Youngling	A child

There's nothin' an underling likes better than a good belly-bungling joke or two. Here're a few old favourites ...

Q: What's Clod's favourite flavour of crisp?
A: Toe cheese and bunion

Q: What's grey-green and invisible?
A: No trolls

Q: Why is Rubella a lot like London fog?
A: Because she's grey-green and thick

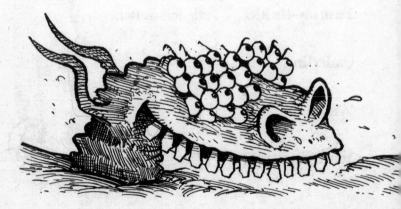

Q: What do you give Malaria
when she's feeling a bit blurty?
A: Plenty of room

Q: What's a slurch's favourite opera?
A: Wriggle-etto

Clod's Fishing Song

When my belly's squinched
And I start to drool
I head off to the fishing pool.
Where the sewer fish meet,
And the eels are sweet
And the gloopy mud is thick and cool.

Then by the twisty weeds I'll wait
With rod and string and hook and worm.
I've picked the wriggliest kind of bait
Cos fishes love it when they squirm.

Oh, to crunch the juicy eye
Of a squibbly great big lumper.
I slurp the scales,
And grunch the tails
And keep on getting plumper.
Or maybe chew the salty skins
Of a slippery eel or two.
They taste of rust and other things
That end up down the loo.

And when I'm done a-fishing
I'll pack my rod and then
I'll glump off home but soon return
And do it all AGAIN . . .

'Ello, my lumps. Since you're probably droolin' and slobber-gobbing after reading a story that's so full of my lummy cooking, I thought you might like some of my recipes to try back at home. I've switched one or two skwinsy ingredients for things you overlings seem to like eatin' so you can grunch away till you're chubbier than a chunkling and cosier than a bungle's bundle.

Malaria

Dungle Droppings

You will need:

- A whopping great 100g bar of chocolate (milk or dark)
- 3 tablespoonfuls of something sweet and sticky . . . maple syrup, honey, or golden syrup should do the trick
- 60g of unsalted butter
- 90g of cereal (This is a good chance to go on a grab around the kitchen. You can use any type of cereal as long as it's flaky, lumpy, crispy and a right tummy-tinkler. You can even mix up lots of different types.)
- A handful of raisins and flaked almonds (if you like but they're not essential)
- About twelve cupcake cases

What's next?

- Get a grown-up to help you melt the chocolate in a bowl over a saucepan of hot water.

- Add the butter and stir until it melts into the chocolate.
- Add the sticky, sweet ingredient (whichever one you chose).
- Finally stir in the cereal until it's all coated in squibbly chocolate.
- When it's all jumbled up nicely, pop a great big spoonful of the stuff into cupcake cases and, if you want to, decorate them with flies made from a raisin with two flaked almond wings.
- Leave them to cool in the fridge and then grunch away. Lummy!

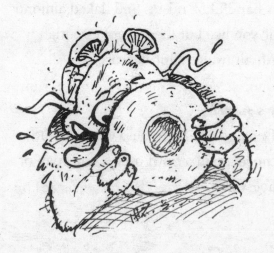

Worms in Dirt

This one is really easy but extra squibbly for parties.

You will need:

- A handful of your favourite biscuits (digestives work the best)
- A pack of chocolate custard from the supermarket
- Some jelly worm sweets from the sweetshop
- About six short, glass tumblers

What's next?

- Get a grown-up to help you make the chocolate custard following the instructions on the back of the packet.
- Crumble the biscuits and split the crumbs into two piles.
- Fill the bottom of the tumblers with the crumbs from one pile.
- Next, pour in some chocolate custard on top of the biscuit crumbs.

🦑 Divide the second pile of crumbs on top of each glass of custard and put the filled glasses in the fridge until the custard is cool and firm.

🦑 Finally add a few jelly worms to the top of each one, then grab a spoon and guzzle. They're the tastiest worms you'll ever eat!

Pickled Fish Eyes

You will need:
- ☉ A handful of cherry tomatoes
  (about five or six)
- ☉ A blunking great load of small
  mozzarella balls (about ten)
- ☉ A few basil leaves
- ☉ Some black olives (about five)

What's next?
- ☉ Cut the cherry tomatoes in half and
  scoop out the seeds with a teaspoon.
- ☉ Pop a mozzarella ball into each of the
  half tomatoes. (You can trim the edges
  of the cheese to make them fit a
  little snugglier.)
- ☉ Get a grown-up to help you carefully
  cut the basil leaves into little circles
  (about the size of a one-penny coin)
  and press them on to the top of each
  mozzarella ball.

- Then chop the olives into little bits to make the pupil and press one into the middle of each basil-leaf circle.
- And there you have it . . . a lummy, squishy eyeball. You can eat them on their own or serve a few on top of some tomatoey pasta. Mmmmmmmmmm . . .

Turn over for a sneak peek of the next

WRONG PONG adventure!

A Note

Neville stared, wide eyed, into the toilet bowl. His mouth twitched into a smile and the hairs on the back of his neck stood on end.

There, floating on the surface of the water, was a single square of toilet tissue. On it in scruffy handwriting were the words 'Nev . . . Fancied a squibbly trolliday . . . We're coming to stay.'